This month, in
REMEMBERING ONE WILD NIGHT
by Kathie DeNosky

Meet Travis Whelan—a jet-setting attorney…
and a *father?* When Natalie Perez showed
up in his life again with the baby daughter
he'd never known about, Travis knew he had
a duty to both of them. But could he find a
way to make them a family?

**SILHOUETTE DESIRE
IS PROUD TO PRESENT THE**

TEXAS
Cattleman's Club
The Stolen Baby

Six wealthy Texas bachelors—all members of the
state's most exclusive club—must unravel the
mystery surrounding one tiny baby…and
discover true love in the process!

* * *

And don't miss
BREATHLESS FOR THE BACHELOR
by Cindy Gerard
The fourth installment of the
Texas Cattleman's Club: The Stolen Baby series.

Available next month in Silhouette Desire!

Dear Reader,

Welcome to another compelling month of powerful, passionate and provocative love stories from Silhouette Desire. You asked for it…you got it…more Dynasties! Our newest continuity, DYNASTIES: THE DANFORTHS, launches this month with Barbara McCauley's *The Cinderella Scandal.* Set in Savannah, Georgia, and filled with plenty of family drama and sensuality, this new twelve-book series will thrill you for the entire year.

There is one sexy air force pilot to be found between the pages of the incomparable Merline Lovelace's *Full Throttle,* part of her TO PROTECT AND DEFEND series. And the fabulous Justine Davis is back in Silhouette Desire with *Midnight Seduction,* a fiery tale in her REDSTONE, INCORPORATED series.

If it's a whirlwind Vegas wedding you're looking for (and who isn't?) then be sure to pick up the third title in Katherine Garbera's KING OF HEARTS miniseries, *Let It Ride.* The fabulous TEXAS CATTLEMAN'S CLUB: THE STOLEN BABY series continues this month with Kathie DeNosky's tale of unforgettable passion, *Remembering One Wild Night.* And finally, welcome new author Amy Jo Cousins to the Desire lineup with her superhot contribution, *At Your Service.*

I hope all of the Silhouette Desire titles this month will fulfill your every fantasy.

Melissa Jeglinski

Melissa Jeglinski
Senior Editor, Silhouette Desire

Please address questions and book requests to:
Silhouette Reader Service
U.S.: 3010 Walden Ave., P.O. Box 1325, Buffalo, NY 14269
Canadian: P.O. Box 609, Fort Erie, Ont. L2A 5X3

Remembering
One Wild Night

KATHIE DeNOSKY

Published by Silhouette Books

America's Publisher of Contemporary Romance

Special thanks and acknowledgment are given to
Kathie DeNosky for her contribution to the
TEXAS CATTLEMAN'S CLUB series.

To the talented ladies of this TEXAS CATTLEMAN'S CLUB
series—Sara Orwig, Laura Wright, Cindy Gerard,
Cathleen Galitz and Kristi Gold. You're the best!

 SILHOUETTE BOOKS

ISBN 0-373-76559-2

REMEMBERING ONE WILD NIGHT

Books by Kathie DeNosky

Silhouette Desire

Did You Say Married?! #1296
The Rough and Ready Rancher #1355
His Baby Surprise #1374
Maternally Yours #1418
Cassie's Cowboy Daddy #1439
Cowboy Boss #1457
A Lawman in Her Stocking #1475
In Bed with the Enemy #1521
Lonetree Ranchers: Brant #1528
Lonetree Ranchers: Morgan #1540
Lonetree Ranchers: Colt #1551
Remembering One Wild Night #1559

Silhouette Books

Home for the Holidays
"New Year's Baby"

KATHIE DeNOSKY

lives in her native southern Illinois with her husband and one very spoiled Jack Russell terrier. She writes highly sensual stories with a generous amount of humor. Kathie's books have appeared on the Waldenbooks bestseller list and received the Write Touch Readers' Award from WisRWA and the National Readers' Choice Award. She enjoys going to rodeos, traveling to research settings for her books and listening to country music. Readers may contact Kathie at P.O. Box 2064, Herrin, Illinois 62948-5264 or e-mail her at kathie@kathiedenosky.com.

"What's Happening in Royal?"

NEWS FLASH, January—Just back from his trip overseas, jet-setter Travis Whelan is just what the doctor ordered for Ms. Jane Doe—or should we say, Ms. Natalie Perez. It seems Royal's most notorious amnesia patient had started to regain her memory! Tongues were set wagging when Trav whisked Natalie off in the middle of the annual TCC New Year's bash. Perhaps Trav and Natalie are more than simply old acquaintances?

Uh-oh, ladies, could another sexy Cattleman be off the market soon? Looks like our resolute bachelor is a daddy! Natalie and her little girl are going to need a tough Texan like Trav to watch over them, because whoever is stalking Natalie is getting meaner and far too close for comfort….

On the lighter side of things, seems like Trav's sister, Carrie Whelan, has her own New Year's resolution to put some romance in her life. And she's set her sights on the new doctor in town! Dr. Belden has kept himself out of the limelight and wouldn't even talk to any of our field reporters, but we hear that he's handsome and single. Good luck nabbing this one, Carrie!

One

When Travis Whelan stepped off the Learjet with fellow Texas Cattleman's Club member Sheik Darin ibn Shakir at the private airstrip just outside of Royal, Texas, he wanted three things—a hot shower, a cold beer and a week's worth of uninterrupted sleep. Was he going to get them?

Hell, no. He and Darin had been invited to David Sorrenson's ranch for a New Year's Eve party. But the carefully worded invitation that had been waiting for them when they arrived at the airfield hadn't fooled either one of the them. David's party wasn't the reason they'd been summoned. Trav and Darin both knew the TCC had another high priority case.

"Did the message indicate what's up?" Trav asked

the stoic figure seated on the passenger side of his dark silver SUV.

"The directive did not say," Darin answered, staring straight ahead.

"It has to be something pretty damn important if it can't wait until we meet the day after tomorrow for the Obersbourg debriefing," Trav said, turning the Mountaineer onto the road that would take them to the TX S Ranch.

Darin gave a short, unemotional nod. "It would appear to be so."

Surprised, Trav glanced at the man. Darin was in an unusually talkative mood, which wasn't saying much, considering the man normally limited his responses to no more than a word or two, and then only when directly addressed. Otherwise, he remained silent—a solitary figure whose demeanor was as dark and foreboding as the black clothing he always wore.

In the two months they'd been working together to find the assassin trying to kill members of the royal family of Obersbourg, Trav had come to know the mysterious, brooding sheik as well, if not better, than any of the other TCC members. And that wasn't much. All Trav knew for sure about Darin was that the man drank enough coffee each day to bleed black if he cut himself shaving, wanted absolutely nothing to do with the trappings of his own royal heritage and preferred working cases alone.

Steering the SUV onto the driveway leading up to the main house at the TX S Ranch, Trav yawned and checked the digital clock on the dashboard. With any luck, he could find out about the club's next mission, get one of the other guys to drive Darin home and be in bed an hour before the beginning of the New Year.

It wasn't the way most people in the good town of Royal would expect their jet-setting, playboy prosecutor to ring in another year. But they were only looking at the carefully crafted facade that Trav had fabricated for his undercover work with the TCC, and not the real man beneath the surface.

He almost laughed out loud at how far from the truth the persona really was. Only his younger sister, Carrie, and best friend, Ryan Evans, knew the true extent of the ruse. Trav was basically a good old boy at heart, much more comfortable in jeans and a work shirt than a suit and tie. And more times than not, his Saturday nights were spent vegging out on the couch in his family room with a bag of popcorn, a cold beer and an old movie playing on his big-screen TV. Alone.

As he thought about watching the vintage films, an image of the woman who had gotten him interested in them came to mind. How was she spending her New Year's Eve? Was she watching her favorite classic movie in the arms of another man?

His gut twisted at the thought and he had to remind himself that it was ancient history. Things hadn't worked out between them, and spending time thinking about it wasn't going to change that fact. Natalie

Perez had made it perfectly clear that if she never set eyes on him again it would be all too soon.

Parking the truck among a variety of vehicles ranging from a sporty little Jaguar to a couple of boxy-looking Hummers, he got out of the Mountaineer with Darin and walked toward the house. Music and laughter greeted them, growing louder the closer they got to the front door.

Trav yawned again as he pressed the doorbell. As soon as one of the guys filled him and Darin in on what was going on, he was out of here. He might even forgo the cold beer, but nothing was going to keep him from that hot shower and his king-size bed. Whatever the new mission was, it was just going to have to wait until tomorrow morning for them to get started on it.

When the door opened, David Sorrenson grinned at Trav and Darin. "We were taking bets on when you two would finally show up."

"Well, hello to you, too, Sorrenson," Trav said, laughing as he and Darin entered the stylish, modern ranch house. "So who won?"

"I'm pretty sure it was Kent." David fished a small piece of paper from his shirt pocket. Glancing at it, he nodded. "Yeah, Alex Kent had the times between nine and ten."

"Who is it, David?" an attractive, petite blonde asked, walking up to stand beside him.

Sorrenson slipped his arm around the woman's

waist, then bent his head to kiss her like a soldier returning from war.

Trav glanced over at Darin about the same time the sheik looked at him. The corners of Darin's mouth turned up slightly in a rare smile, surprising Trav further.

What the hell was going on? When their flight cut across the Bermuda Triangle on the trip home from Obersbourg, had he been thrown into the Twilight Zone and failed to notice the fact?

Darin had been talkative. David was showing the little blonde more affection than Trav had ever seen him show any woman in front of the guys. And now the sheik was smiling?

"Honey, this is Travis Whelan and Sheik Darin ibn Shakir," David said, grinning like the cat that swallowed the canary. "Travis, Darin, I'd like you to meet my wife, Marissa."

"Your wife?" Trav asked incredulously.

David nodded. "And, hopefully this time next year, the mother of my baby."

Now Trav knew he was stuck in the Twilight Zone. David Sorrenson had always insisted he wasn't cut out for marriage and definitely wasn't father material.

"Congratulations," Trav finally managed to exclaim, getting over his initial shock. "What else has changed since we've been gone?"

"Andover got married a couple of days ago," David answered, clearly enjoying Trav's astonishment. "He's honeymooning in Europe now."

"The hell you say." Chuckling, Trav shook his head. "Anybody else we know join the ranks of the blissfully hitched?"

"Not yet." David laughed. "But who knows, you or Darin could be the next TCC member to take a trip down the aisle."

Trav held up both hands defensively. "Not me. I'm not the marrying kind."

"What about you, Darin?" David asked, smiling.

"No." The sheik's answer was simple, but the timbre of his voice and the look in his obsidian eyes held a wealth of meaning.

Before anyone could recover from the vehemence in Darin's one-word response, Ryan Evans walked over to join the group standing in the foyer. "Hey, Trav, it's about damn time you showed up. You cost me twenty-five bucks tonight. If you'd just gotten here an hour earlier, I'd have won the pool."

"Hey, Ry." Trav gave his best friend a brotherly hug and clapped him on the back. "So what's been going on with you, besides losing another bet? You didn't get hitched while we were away, did you?"

Ry snorted. "A jackass will fly first."

David laughed. "I'm going to let Evans bring you two up to speed," he said, turning to join the rest of his guests. "I need to let Alex know he won the bet and pay him his winnings."

As David and his wife moved away, Ry motioned for the new arrivals to follow him over to the bar that had been set up across the room. "Come on, let's grab a long-neck and I'll fill you in."

Accepting the tall, amber-colored bottle from the man David had hired to tend bar for the evening, Trav tipped it back and drank. He had the cold one he'd been wanting; now all he needed was the shower and a good night's sleep.

"Before you start telling me about this new case, I want to know if Carrie's all right." He looked around. "Is she here tonight?"

"Your sister?" Darin asked, taking a swig of the black coffee he'd requested from the bartender.

Trav nodded. "Trying to keep track of her is almost a full-time job."

Ry snorted and turned to Darin. "Yeah, and while you two were in Obersbourg, he left me to baby-sit." He smiled and rocked back on his heels. "But I got a reprieve tonight. She and her friend Stephanie Firth are chaperoning some high school dance or something."

Laughing, Trav nodded. "But I see you survived the ordeal."

"Carrie-bear wasn't happy about me checking up on her all the time," Ry said, his brown eyes dancing. "But I can say with one hundred and fifty percent certainty that she's still as pure as the day you left for Obersbourg." He took a drink of his beer. "But I'm damn glad you're home. You can watch out for her now. She's set her sights on the new doctor in town and she's hell-bent on learning everything she can about him.''

''What's this guy's name? What do you know about him? And has he already taken Carrie out?'' Trav fired the questions at Ry like bullets from a gun, not at all happy with what his friend was telling him.

''Nathan Beldon is the guy's name, but that's about all anyone knows about him.'' Ry reached for a handful of peanuts from a dish on the bar. ''He keeps to himself and won't attend parties or anything else he's invited to. And that's bugging the hell out of Carrie-bear. She hasn't met him yet, but not from lack of trying.''

''I don't care how friendly or antisocial this joker is, just as long as he steers clear of her,'' Trav said, frowning.

''How old is your sister?'' Darin asked.

''She's twenty-four.'' Trav shook his head. ''But she's way too naive to get involved with some slick doctor I don't know anything about.''

The sheik nodded as if he understood Trav's cautionary attitude about his only sister, then turned his attention to Ry. ''What is so crucial about our next case?''

Ry's expression instantly turned grim. ''It's the damnedest thing. Back in early November, when the guys got together for the monthly chili-fest, this woman stumbled into the Royal Diner. Her clothes were muddy and torn, her head was bleeding and she was holding a brand-new baby girl.''

Getting ready to take another swallow of beer, Trav froze with his hand halfway to his mouth. His gut clenched painfully as he slowly lowered the bottle. "Domestic battery?"

"Actually, that wasn't even a consideration," Ry said, popping a peanut into his mouth. "Just before she collapsed, she begged David not to let 'them' take her baby."

"To whom did she refer?" Darin asked, his dark eyes blazing over the edge of his coffee cup as he took another sip.

"We don't know. She's had amnesia ever since." Frowning, Ry placed his empty beer bottle on the table. "But whoever clunked her on the head did a good job of it. She was in a coma for a week, and when she finally woke up, she didn't even realize she'd had a baby."

"What do the doctors say?" Trav asked, wondering what the TCC could do to help the woman.

"The neurologist said her memory could come back all at once, or in bits and pieces." Ry paused. "Or there's a possibility that she'll never remember anything before waking up in the hospital." He turned to look around the crowded room. "She's here somewhere."

Darin motioned for the bartender to refill his coffee cup. "Where is the baby?"

"David and Marissa took care of her while Jane was in the hospital," Ry answered. "After Jane was discharged, she insisted the baby remain here with them. She said she thought it would be safer, and we all agreed she was probably right.''

Trav cocked an eyebrow. "Jane?"

"Jane Doe is what we've been calling her," Ry said, shrugging. He turned to face Trav. "She was staying with Tara Roberts before someone started to send threatening letters and then ended up torching Tara's house. Jane and the baby are both staying here with David and Marissa for now."

Trav swore. "Whoever it is she's running from is obviously still after her."

Ry nodded. "Someone tried to kidnap the baby when Marissa visited Jane in the hospital. Fortunately, Marissa was able to get away from the thug and she did get a description of him." He gave Trav and Darin a meaningful look. "Then there's the little matter of the five hundred thousand dollars that Jane had tucked inside the baby's diaper bag the night she showed up at the diner. She can't remember why she was carrying that kind of money around, or where she got it. And there were no clues in the bag to give us anything to go on."

Trav gave a low whistle. He noticed that even the normally impassive sheik stopped swigging coffee to stare wide-eyed at Ry.

"How did she get hold of us?" Trav asked, handing his empty beer bottle to the bartender. He shook his head when the man moved to get him another.

"They found a crumpled Texas Cattleman's Club card in her hand just before the ambulance got to the diner that night." He motioned for Trav and Darin to follow him. "Come on, I'll introduce you to her."

"Who gave her the card?" Trav asked, wondering if they could trace her identity that way.

"Nobody seems to know," Ry said, walking toward the kitchen.

Trav wondered how the TCC could help the woman. If she couldn't remember who she was, who was after her or why, there wasn't a whole lot the members could do but keep her and her baby safe until whoever was chasing her tipped his hand. But then, that was what the Texas Cattleman's Club was all about. Leadership, Justice and Peace was the motto all the members lived by.

And if anyone needed peace and justice, it seemed this woman did.

When Jane heard the doorbell chime, she anxiously glanced around the room full of happy people. This might be the opportunity she'd been waiting for. Everyone's attention seemed to be directed toward the two men who had just arrived for David and Marissa Sorrenson's New Year's Eve party.

Rising to her feet, she turned and walked calmly but purposefully down the hall. She didn't wait to see who the late arrivals were. It didn't matter. She wouldn't know them, anyway.

Jane sighed heavily. She didn't even know who she was and it was beginning to look as if she never would.

But whatever her name was, it was clear she was putting those around her in danger. Some of them had already received threatening letters, and Tara had even lost her home because Jane had been staying with her.

Jane would always be grateful for their kindness and generosity, but she refused to jeopardize their safety any longer. That's why she'd come to the agonizing decision that it was time for her and her baby daughter, Autumn, to leave Royal, Texas.

Entering the room she'd been sharing with the baby since Tara's house had been destroyed by an arsonist, Jane quickly wrote a note thanking everyone for their help. Then, gathering her daughter's things, she placed them in a bag, put her jacket on and wrapped the baby in a warm blanket. Careful not to wake Autumn, Jane picked her up and walked quickly down the hall.

She'd take the back way to the kitchen to avoid being seen, get a couple of bottles of formula from the refrigerator, then slip out the back door undetected. With any luck, she'd be well on her way before anyone noticed they were missing or found the note explaining why she'd made the decision to leave.

Once she had the baby bottles tucked inside the new diaper bag Marissa had given her, she started for the door. But just as she put her hand on the polished brass knob, a male voice stopped her in her tracks.

''Jane, I've got a couple more TCC members I'd

like you to meet,'' Ryan Evans said from behind her. ''Hey, where are you going?''

She heard the confusion in his voice, and, slowly turning to face him, tried to think of an excuse for why she would be taking the baby outside at such a late hour. ''I thought I would—''

Noticing the man standing beside Ryan, she stopped abruptly. There was something very familiar about him. Nearly an inch shorter than Ryan's six foot height, he had light brown hair, hazel eyes and…

''Natalie,'' the man said incredulously, taking a step toward her.

She opened her mouth to ask him why he'd called her by that name, but with sudden, blinding clarity she knew. Her name was Natalie—Natalie Perez. She was twenty-five years old and lived in Chicago.

Blinking, she watched the handsome man take a step toward her. His name was Travis Whelan. He was thirty-two, a millionaire and…

Her head began to throb as realization slammed into her with the force of a physical blow. He wasn't just someone she'd once known.

Travis Whelan was her baby's father, and the man she'd sworn she never wanted to see again.

Two

Natalie's head pounded unmercifully as the room seemed to spin out of control. Her vision began to close in from the sides as if a dark curtain was being drawn, and she knew she was going to pass out. Holding the baby close, she dropped the diaper bag and blindly reached for something to hang on to in an attempt to keep from falling.

"She's going down!" she heard Ryan shout. His voice sounded desperate, and it barely registered with her when he and Travis both lunged for her.

She felt someone take Autumn from her at the same moment two strong arms swept her up to cradle her to a wide, masculine chest. "I've got you, Natalie," Travis said, his deep baritone sending a shock wave throughout her entire system. "You're going to be all right."

She heard Autumn begin to wail at the top of her little lungs. "My...b-baby," Natalie managed to say, concerned more for her daughter than for herself.

"She's fine." Travis's warm breath stirred the hair at her temple, sending goose bumps over every inch of her skin. "Ry and Darin will take good care of her, darlin'."

Her strength returned in slow degrees as the shock of seeing Travis again, and the realization that she'd remembered parts of her past, began to subside. "P-please put me down," she said, hating that her voice sounded shaky and vulnerable.

"Not yet, darlin'." The gentle tone of Travis's voice sent another shiver streaking up her spine.

"I...I can walk," she insisted.

He shook his head. "It would be best if you put your feet up for a few minutes."

"What's going on?" David asked as he entered the kitchen. "I thought I heard Ryan shout something about someone falling."

"Natalie came close to passing out," Travis answered. "I think it would be a good idea if she lay down for a while. Where's her room?"

"Natalie?" David sounded confused.

"Her room is down the hall," Marissa said from behind her husband.

Embarrassed more than she'd ever been in her life, Natalie wished they'd all just go away and forget she existed. "I—I'm fine. Really." She tried one last time. "I just have a slight headache."

But Travis ignored her protests and followed Marissa down the hall toward the room she'd been sharing with Autumn. When he'd gently laid her on the bed, he sat down beside her and took her hand in his. "Do you remember who I am, Natalie?"

As she gazed up at him, images of them together flashed through her mind. Travis meeting her at the diner where she worked as a waitress. Travis laughing with her while they ate popcorn and watched videos in her modest apartment. And Travis holding her, loving her with a tenderness that still caused her breath to catch.

Then, just as swiftly, the memory of his deception came rushing forward. Her head pounded as she relived the hurt and anger she'd felt when she'd found he wasn't who he'd portrayed himself to be.

He'd told her he was a cowboy from west Texas who had come to Chicago looking for something to do other than eat dust herding cattle, and that they shared the same kind of modest upbringing. But that had been the furthest thing from the truth. When he'd inadvertently left his ID at her apartment, she'd learned there was nothing about his background that could even remotely be considered common. He was not only a successful prosecuting attorney, but a multimillionaire.

"Natalie, do you know who I am, darlin'?" he repeated, gently brushing a strand of hair from her cheek.

"Y-yes, I remember you," she answered, closing her eyes. The concern she saw in the depths of his hazel gaze was probably nothing more than an illusion.

"Do you know who you are?" he asked, continuing to question her.

"Yes. I'm Natalie Perez."

"Can you remember what happened, darlin'? Or why you came to Texas?" he asked, his voice so tender it sent another shiver up her spine.

She opened her eyes to stare at him. "I…" She stopped to think. But as hard as she tried, she couldn't recall why she'd come to Royal, Texas. "I can't remember. I…just knew I had to get here."

"Travis, could we talk to you for a minute?" David asked from behind him.

Trav turned to see David, Darin, Alex Kent and a nervous looking Ry—still holding the crying baby—standing just outside the door. Turning back to Natalie, Trav gave her what he hoped was a reassuring smile. "I'll be right back, darlin'."

Rising to his feet, he waited until Marissa Sorrenson took his place beside Natalie before he joined the group of men in the hall.

Alex Kent, another member of the TCC, was the first to speak. "Ryan told us you know Jane. He said her name is Natalie."

Trav nodded. "I met her when I worked that case in Chicago last year."

"Well, that explains who gave her our card," David said, raising his voice enough to be heard above the crying infant.

"Before we start hashing out who knows who, could we get one of the women to take this baby?" Ry asked, looking more uncomfortable by the second. "I don't have a clue how to make her stop screeching."

"But you're the ladies' man," Alex said, grinning. "You've always led us to believe that you know exactly what a female wants and how to make her happy."

"Yeah, but that's with women over the age of twenty-one," Ry said. His face flushed a dull red. "I don't know a damn thing about females under that age." When the baby took a breath and started howling with renewed vigor, he grimaced. "And to tell you the truth, I really don't care to learn."

"Here, let me have Autumn," Marissa said, hurrying out into the hall to take the infant from Ry. When she lifted the baby to her shoulder, the child immediately stopped squalling.

Trav glanced at the baby raising such a ruckus. He supposed she was cute as babies went. She had light brown hair and a little cowlick on the left side of her forehead. His scalp tingled when Marissa stuck a pacifier in the baby's mouth and tiny dimples appeared in her chubby little cheeks.

"Who is the woman and how did you come to know her, Travis?" Darin asked, steering the conversation back to the business at hand, as well as distracting Trav from his perusal of the infant.

He glanced back through the open door at the woman lying on the bed. Eleven months ago, Natalie Perez had been the only bright spot in his otherwise dismal two-month stay in the Windy City.

After a particularly difficult day on the case he'd been working for the TCC, he'd gone for a walk to clear his head, and had ended up wandering into a little diner not far from the apartment he'd rented. Natalie had been waiting tables, and from the moment she came over to take his order he'd been entranced. Everything about her had appealed to him. Her sweet smile, the slightly husky quality to her velvet voice and the lithe way her slender body moved as she waited on the other customers had fascinated the hell out of him. He'd ended up walking her home that evening after she got off work, and it had been the beginning of their month-long involvement.

Unfortunately, due to working undercover and the sensitive nature of his mission in Chicago, he'd been unable to share much of anything important about himself. When she'd discovered that he wasn't the man he'd led her to believe he was, she'd been deeply hurt by his deception and had immediately ended things between them.

But before he walked out of her apartment for the last time, he'd given her the TCC card and told her that if she ever needed to get in touch with him, to use the address on the card. Shortly after that he'd brought his mission in Chicago to a successful end and returned to Royal. But he'd never been able to forget her, or the feelings she'd aroused in him.

"Her name is Natalie Perez. She and I were…friends for about a month during my stay in Chicago last year," Trav said, choosing his words carefully. The extent of his relationship with Natalie was nobody's business but their own. "When I left, I gave her one of our business cards and told her that if she ever wanted to get hold of me, she could reach me through the TCC."

"I'm surprised she hung on to it that long," David said, shaking his head in obvious amazement. "It's been the better part of a year, hasn't it?"

"Eleven months," Trav said, nodding as he glanced back at the bed. His scalp suddenly started to tingle once again when he saw Natalie sit up and reach for the infant. "How old did you say that baby is?" he asked.

"Jane—er, Natalie—can't remember what day the baby was born," Alex Kent said, glancing into the bedroom. "But when we got Justin Webb to examine her the night they showed up at the diner, he said she couldn't have been more than a day or two old."

Feeling as if his hair was standing straight up, Trav turned to Ry. "And you said that was two months ago?"

Ry nodded. "Yeah. Why?"

Trav mentally calculated the time span, then counted again. Without answering Ry, he walked back into the bedroom.

"Marissa, could you give Natalie and me a moment alone?"

"Of course," the woman said. Walking out of the room, she pulled the door shut behind her.

"Could I see her?" Trav asked, holding his arms out to take the baby.

Natalie's violet eyes were wary, but without a word she handed him the infant.

Cradling the baby girl to his chest, Trav swallowed hard as he stared down at her. The cowlick at the hairline on the left side of the baby's forehead was just like the one all Whelans had, and the dimples were tiny, but looked much like those denting his own cheeks.

He turned his attention to Natalie, and watched the caution in her pretty eyes change to abject resignation. His heart hammered against his rib cage so hard it wouldn't have surprised him if it cracked a couple of ribs.

"She's mine, isn't she?" he asked, already knowing the answer.

Natalie stared at him for several long seconds before raising her chin a notch and squaring her slender shoulders. "Yes."

Even though Trav had expected her to confirm his suspicions, he still felt as if he'd been run over by the Dallas Cowboys' entire defensive line. He had a child—a baby daughter—and someone was threatening her and her mother.

A myriad of emotions swept through him, the least of which was a protectiveness so fierce it made him weak in the knees. Although it had been several years since his hand-to-hand combat training in the Marine Corps, he could still be one mean son of a bitch when he had to be. And whoever was causing trouble for his little girl and her mother would have to come through him before they got within spitting distance of either one of them.

Handing the baby back to Natalie, Travis found his initial shock was quickly changing to anger. He had about a thousand questions he wanted answered, the first one being why she'd failed to get in touch with him as soon as she discovered she was pregnant.

But now wasn't the time to start interrogating her. She wasn't up to it, and he needed to calm down before he lost his cool completely.

"I'll send David's wife in to help you pack all of yours and the baby's things," he said, making a snap decision.

"W-why?" Her expression indicated that she was more than a little apprehensive.

He started for the door, then turned back to face her. "You and Autumn will be staying with me from now on."

Her long, dark brown hair swayed from side to side as she shook her head. "No, we're not."

Trav ignored the panic in her expressive eyes as he folded his arms across his chest. "Yes, you are."

"But—"

"No buts about it, Natalie. You and my daughter are going home with me." He smiled, but he doubted he looked very friendly or accommodating. "We need time to sort through everything that's happened to you, as well as to come to some kind of agreement about Autumn."

Before she could argue the point further, Trav turned and went back out into the hall, where the group of men and Sorrenson's wife still stood. "Marissa, could you go in and help Natalie pack? I'm taking her and my daughter home with me."

A shocked silence reigned as everyone digested his unexpected announcement.

Looking as if he'd been treated to the business end of a cattle prod, Ry was the first to regain his voice. "Your what?"

"My *daughter*," Trav answered calmly, surprised at how easily the word rolled off his tongue, and how good it felt to let his friends know he was her daddy.

"*You're* the baby's father?" Alex asked, clearly shocked.

Trav nodded. "I still don't know the particulars, but Natalie was obviously trying to find me when she came to Royal."

"It does make more sense for her to stay out at your ranch," David said, looking thoughtful. "It's just a matter of time before whoever's after them figures out they're staying here.''

Ry nodded. ''You've been out of the country since they arrived in Royal, and no one would think to look at the Flying W.''

''I agree,'' Alex said.

''It would be best for you to take them with you tonight, under the cover of darkness,'' Darin added pragmatically.

''That's what I figure.'' Trav turned to Ry. ''Could you keep an eye on Carrie for a few more days, while I get things sorted out?''

''Sure.'' Ry still looked like a kid who'd just stuck his finger in a light socket. ''What do you want me to tell Carrie-bear?''

''Don't tell her anything for now,'' Trav said, deciding caution would be the best way to handle the situation. He knew he'd have to tell his sister soon, but he needed time to get Natalie and the baby settled, then get some much needed answers before he faced the third degree from Carrie-bear.

''So it's decided,'' David said, finalizing the plan. ''While you keep Natalie and the baby safe at the Flying W, the rest of us will continue the investigation and see if we can't flush out whoever is posing the threat.''

Trav nodded. ''I'll see what I can do to help Natalie regain her memory, and report anything that might help the case.''

* * *

Natalie glanced at the man driving the big silver SUV through the quiet west Texas night. When she'd recognized Travis this evening in David and Marissa's kitchen, she'd fleetingly wondered why she hadn't contacted him when she'd discovered she was pregnant. But as the evening wore on, she remembered all too clearly why she'd chosen to keep her pregnancy a secret.

When they had met last year, she'd fallen head over heels in love with him. But all too soon she'd discovered that he couldn't be trusted. Aside from the fact that he'd lied to her, he was a millionaire. And she'd learned the hard way that wealthy people used others for their own gains, then tossed them aside as if they were completely expendable.

A cold chill shook her body. A baby could be raised without its mother. Did Travis consider her expendable now that he knew about their daughter? What had he meant when he'd mentioned an agreement about Autumn? Was he going to try to take her child from her?

Unlike Natalie, he certainly had the money to fight a lengthy legal battle. And being a county prosecutor, he probably had more than enough connections to get a friendly judge to go along with whatever he wanted.

Desperation began to claw at her insides. What had she been thinking when she'd made her way to Royal? Hadn't she given a thought to what Travis might do when he discovered Autumn was his daughter?

Natalie nervously glanced at his handsome profile. Before she let Travis take her baby away from her, he'd have to find her. At the first opportunity, she fully intended to leave his ranch and Royal, Texas, as far behind as possible.

"I don't want you to worry about your or the baby's safety while you're at the Flying W," Travis said, steering the Mountaineer onto a narrow road. "My ranch is pretty secluded, and if that isn't enough of a deterrent, there's always Fluffy."

Natalie frowned. She didn't like the idea that the ranch was so far from town. That would make leaving all the more difficult.

"Is Fluffy your dog?" she asked cautiously. She didn't think she'd mind a small dog, but the thought of a large one frightened her.

Travis nodded. "As long as he's around nobody wanders onto the property or gets out of a vehicle unless he knows them."

"His name doesn't exactly incite fear," she said, hoping that the animal was as nonthreatening as it implied.

The rich sound of Travis's low chuckle sent a wave of goose bumps up her arms. "Trust me. Once you see Fluffy, you won't have any doubts about his ability to intimidate just about anyone."

They'd ridden in silence for several minutes when

Natalie noticed lights in the distance. "Is that your ranch up ahead?"

He nodded. "That's it."

There weren't any other lights for miles, and Natalie's hopes of finding a way to leave without Travis's knowledge all but disintegrated. It truly was isolated, and when they turned off the main road onto the long lane leading up to the house, she conceded that she didn't have any other option but to stay and hope for the best. Besides, it was obvious that, although she couldn't remember who she was running from, she'd been trying to reach Travis. She just wished with all her heart she could remember why.

When he parked the Mountaineer in the circular drive in front of the house, Natalie found herself staring at a beautiful, two-story stucco hacienda. She couldn't tell much about it in the dark, except that it was quite large and had a front courtyard with double wrought-iron gates. Considering his wealth, she wasn't surprised by its size or the ornate entrance.

Before she could get her shoulder belt unfastened, Travis was out of the truck and opening the passenger door for her. "Hey there, Fluffy," he said, turning to pet the biggest dog she'd ever seen. "Did you keep Mose busy while I was gone?"

"My God, that's not a dog, it's a horse." Natalie drew back, not at all sure she wanted to get out of the SUV.

"Don't worry," Travis said, opening the back door

to unstrap the baby's car seat. "You're with me. Fluffy won't bother you."

She eyed the dog warily. "Are you sure?"

Laughing, he nodded. "He's well-trained, and besides, mastiffs aren't mean by nature. They don't have to be. Their size and bark are enough to scare the hell out of most people."

"I'll have to take your word that he isn't mean," she said, keeping an eye on the massive canine. "But I believe you about strangers being out of their minds to come near this place when he's around."

Travis picked up the baby carrier, then placed a hand at the small of her back. "You'll get used to Fluffy. He's a gentle giant. Besides, he spends most of his time with Mose."

She looked around as Travis guided her through the wrought-iron gates. The front courtyard was lovely, with strategically placed landscape lighting to enhance the terra-cotta walkway and native southwest Texas cactus and yucca plants.

"Mose?" she asked, when he stopped to punch numbers into the security system.

"Mose Barringer." When the tiny light went out on the keypad, he unlocked the carved oak door. "He's supposed to be my housekeeper and cook, but don't tell him that."

"Why?" she asked, wondering how many others he employed as household help.

"Because Mose thinks he runs things around here." A knowing look spread across Travis's handsome face. "Once you meet him, you'll see what I mean."

When he opened the door, Fluffy pushed past Natalie and walked right in. Startled, she glanced at Travis, but he didn't act as if that was at all unusual.

"Isn't he rather large to be an inside dog?"

Travis shrugged. "An animal Fluffy's size is an anywhere-he-wants-to-go dog. That's why I had an over-size doggie door installed in the kitchen. He's free to move about as he pleases."

Preceding Travis into the foyer, she looked around while he locked the door and reset the security system. His home was decorated in the traditional Southwest style, with white stucco walls, rich wood trim and bright Mexican and Native American accents.

A big, antique grandfather clock in the foyer chimed eleven times, causing Natalie to glance at it in surprise. "I...didn't realize it was so late," she said, wishing she hadn't sounded so darn breathless. Being with him again made her nervous. "If you'll tell me which room Autumn and I will be sharing, I think I'll get her settled, then turn in for the night."

He stared at her for several seconds before he gave a short nod, then placed his hand at the small of her back again and ushered her to a set of stairs with beautiful oak railings. "As soon as I show you to your room, I'll go out to the truck and get the portable crib."

His hand seemed to burn right through her clothing—jacket, denim jumper and all—to heat her skin and make her feel warm all over. Natalie quickly stepped away from him at the top of the stairs.

"Your home is very nice," she said, unsure of what else to say.

"I had very little to do with the way it looks," he said, shrugging. "All I did was pick out the style of house I wanted to build. Carrie-bear did the decorating."

The name sounded like an endearment, and Natalie found herself wondering if Carrie was his current love interest. Her stomach twisted into a tight knot at the thought, which was ridiculous, all things considered. She wasn't interested in Travis Whelan, or who his girlfriend was.

"In case you're wondering, Carrie-bear—Carrie—is my younger sister," he said, as if he'd read her mind.

"I wasn't. Wondering, that is," Natalie lied. She had been, but he didn't need to know that.

Opening another beautifully carved oak door, he turned on the ceiling fan's light and waited for her to enter. "This is the room Carrie uses when she occasionally stays over."

"Are you sure she won't mind?" Natalie asked, looking around the beautiful bedroom.

The heavy, golden-oak bed had sunbursts intricately carved on the head- and footboard, and a matching dresser, armoire and nightstand completed the bedroom ensemble. A lamp sitting on the nightstand was made from a cream-colored Mexican pot with a mauve and light turquoise Native American design painted on it, and a bright serape hung on one of the white stucco walls. Everything from the pastel, Mexican print comforter with matching pillows, to the picture of an old Spanish mission hanging on the wall above an antique rocking chair, added character to the room and made it feel warm and inviting.

"Carrie-bear won't mind," Travis said, setting Autumn's carrier in the middle of the queen-size bed. "She only uses this room a couple of times a year. Mostly when we get together for special things like Christmas, or my annual Fourth of July barbeque."

"She has a wonderful talent for decorating," Natalie said wistfully.

When she was younger she'd always wanted to decorate the apartment she'd shared with her father in a certain style, with matching accents. But they couldn't afford it. Then, after his death, she'd barely been able to buy the necessities from the thrift store for her much smaller place.

"Are you all right, Natalie?" Travis asked, touching her shoulder.

The feel of his hand, even through her clothing, was like an electric charge. Stepping back, she nodded. "I'm fine."

He stared at her for several long seconds before turning toward the hall. "I'll go down and get the baby bed from the SUV."

When he returned, he quickly set up the portable bed, which David Sorrenson had bought when she and the baby had first arrived in Royal. "Is there anything else you think you or Autumn will need tonight?"

"No, thank you," she said, wishing he'd leave so she could collect herself. His presence was making her feel edgy, as memories of their time together came back to her in bits and pieces.

The faint sound of the grandfather clock chiming twelve times drifted up to them. Travis turned to face her, his gaze holding her captive as he leaned forward. Mesmerized, Natalie stood frozen to the spot, her pulse pounding, her breathing coming in short little puffs.

Her breath caught when he lowered his head, and just when she thought he was going to kiss her, he touched her cheek with his fingertips and whispered close to her ear, "Happy New Year, Natalie. We'll talk in the morning. Good night."

Then, without so much as a backward glance, he walked to the door and quietly closed it behind him.

Three

Lying awake in his king-size bed, Trav found his head aching from tension and lack of sleep. All he'd had on his mind when he and Darin got off the private jet a few hours ago was a cold beer, a hot shower and a good night's sleep. He supposed two out of three wasn't bad. He'd gotten the cold beer at David's last night, and the shower once he'd settled Natalie and the baby in their room across the hall. But sleep wasn't happening, even though he was dead tired and suffering a major case of jet lag.

Glancing at the clock on his bedside table, he decided it wasn't likely he'd get any sleep at all. Dawn was coming and he hadn't so much as nodded off. Hell, how could he? He had too many things running through his mind.

First and foremost was why Natalie hadn't contacted him about her pregnancy. Didn't she think he'd want to know that he'd fathered a baby? Why didn't she want him to be part of Autumn's life?

He realized things between them had ended badly, but that didn't mean he wouldn't love and care for his own child.

Anger swept through him at the thought that if Natalie hadn't found herself in some kind of trouble, he might never have known about his daughter.

And that brought him to the second, and quite possibly the most important question of all. Why were Natalie and the baby being threatened? And by whom?

As angry as he was with Natalie, his stomach churned at the thought of someone harming either one of them. He'd made a vow last night to keep them both safe, and he would walk through hell and back in order to do just that.

Thinking of how best to go about finding out who was threatening them, he decided to extend his leave of absence as the county's prosecuting attorney. He'd taken two months off to go to Obersbourg. What was another few weeks going to hurt?

Fortunately, there wasn't a lot of crime in and around Royal, and he had plenty of time to go on missions for the TCC. But as crucial as those cases had been, guarding Natalie and Autumn was by far his most important objective. First thing Monday morning he'd call and make arrangements for the assistant prosecutor to continue taking care of the office until whoever was posing a danger to them was behind bars.

Trav felt somewhat better just having decided on a plan. Now all he had to do was figure out a way to help Natalie regain her memory. Once they had accomplished that, he'd bet every dime he had they'd know the identity of the bastard trying to harm her and the baby.

As he lay there trying to think of what he could do that might help jog her memory, he heard the faint sound of the baby crying. Several seconds later, Natalie's door opened and he heard her murmuring words of assurance to the child as she walked past his room. He looked at the clock again and decided it was probably time for Autumn's breakfast.

Throwing back the covers, he got out of bed and quickly pulled on a clean pair of jeans, then opened his door and padded barefoot down the hall to the stairs. If Natalie's reaction to Fluffy last night was any indication, she'd lose it completely if she ran across him while getting a bottle of baby formula from the refrigerator.

A feminine shriek, then the sound of the baby wailing at the top of her tiny lungs quickened his steps. As Trav entered the kitchen, he stopped short at the sight before him. With the baby clutched tightly to her breast, Natalie had her back plastered against the front of the refrigerator. Fluffy stood in front of her, looking up at the panicked female with soulful eyes.

When the dog heard Trav, he looked at him as if to ask, "What the hell's wrong with her?"

"Here, Fluffy," Trav said, snapping his fingers. The dog immediately walked over and plopped down at his feet. "Stay."

Turning his attention to the traumatized woman and crying baby, Trav walked over to pull her and his daughter into his arms. The baby immediately stopped crying, and as he held them to his bare chest, he tried to ignore how nice it felt as he tried to calm Natalie.

"It's all right, darlin'. Fluffy wouldn't hurt you or the baby. He's only trying to be friendly."

"What in tarnation is all the danged caterwaulin' about?" Mose grumbled as he limped out of the housekeeper's bedroom just off the kitchen. Wearing nothing but his long johns, he stopped short at the sight of the woman and baby in Trav's arms, his bushy white eyebrows drawn down in a frown. "Is that a youngun'?"

Trav nodded. "Natalie, I'd like you to meet Mose Barringer, the orneriest cowboy turned housekeeper west of the Mississippi. Mose, this is Natalie Perez, and my daughter, Autumn."

The old man's faded blue eyes widened and his whiskered jaw dropped. "What did you say?"

"My daughter," Trav repeated. "Would you like to take a closer look at her *after* you get some clothes on?"

Reminded of what he had on, or more to the point, what he wasn't wearing, Mose turned red from the top of his grizzled beard to his snow-white hairline. Without another word he turned and limped back into his bedroom as fast as his seventy-plus years and arthritis would allow.

Trav grinned. "He's going to give me hell for that."

"What do you mean?" Natalie asked, sounding a little less apprehensive when Fluffy rose to his feet to follow Mose.

Staring down at the woman in his arms, Trav brushed a strand of silky, dark brown hair from her porcelain cheek. "He's going to be mad at me for the rest of the day for calling your attention to the fact that he was in his long underwear."

"I was so frightened by Fluffy, I really didn't notice what he was wearing," she said, shaking her head. "Nor did I care."

Autumn chose that moment to start crying again with renewed vigor.

"Let me hold her while you get her bottle," Trav said, stepping back and stretching out his arms. He wasn't used to holding babies, unless it was the bovine or equine kind, but he fully intended to get acquainted with his daughter whether her mother liked it or not.

Natalie stared at him for a moment before she nodded and placed Autumn in his arms, then pulled her robe close around her. He watched her turn to open the big side-by-side refrigerator, then glance over her shoulder at him as if she didn't trust him.

Trav frowned. She acted as if she thought he and Autumn might disappear if she took her eyes off them.

That's when it hit him. *She's afraid you're going to try to get sole custody.*

"I'll feed the baby while you change clothes," he offered, baiting her to see if his assumption was correct.

When she turned to face him, she was as pale as a ghost. "That won't be necessary. I'll give her a bottle, then take her with me when I go back upstairs to get dressed."

As furious as he was about this, he wanted to put Natalie's mind at ease. She had enough to deal with worrying about some unknown threat to her and the baby. He couldn't, in good conscience, add to her anxiety.

"Natalie, we need to get something straight. I'm angry with you for keeping your pregnancy a secret. And I'm not going to lie to you. I do want joint custody of our daughter. But I'm not going to try to take her away from you. We'll work out a way to share raising her."

He didn't think is was possible, but Natalie's complexion blanched further. Walking over to her, he reached out to cup her cheek with his palm.

"Darlin', contrary to what you believe, I am a man of my word. You can put your trust in what I'm telling you."

She stared at him for several long seconds. He

could tell she was still wary, but finally she nodded, and said, "It will only take me a few minutes to change."

"Good enough," he replied, carrying Autumn over to the table. He pulled out one of the chairs and sat down. "You'll have to show me what to do."

His chest swelled with more emotion than he'd ever dreamed possible at the realization he was actually holding his own child.

"There's really nothing to it," she assured him, sounding less guarded.

"I've never been around a baby, except for my sister. And that was twenty-four years ago." He shrugged. "Eight-year-old boys are more interested in whether or not the fish down at the creek are biting. Or how much farther they can spit than their best friend." He glanced at Natalie. "But I'm going to learn how to take care of Autumn."

In the process of putting the bottle into the microwave to warm the formula, she stopped to frown at him. "I haven't been around babies much, either. I was an only child." Her eyes suddenly widened. "Oh, my. Why hadn't I remembered that before?"

Trav gave her a reassuring smile. "Give it time. It'll all come back to you."

"I hope so." She nibbled on her lower lip a moment as if trying to remember more before she finally set the microwave's timer and pressed the Start button. "It's so frustrating not being able to recall even the simplest of things. Sometimes it feels like whatever I'm trying to remember is just beyond my grasp.''

''I s'pose you two want a cup of joe and somethin' to stuff down your throats for breakfast,'' Mose grumbled when he and Fluffy reentered the kitchen. This time the old codger was dressed in a red plaid flannel shirt, a pair of faded jeans and boots Trav was pretty sure were older than he was.

''After I get dressed, I'll help you, Mr. Barringer,'' Natalie said. Trav watched her give Fluffy a cautious look as she took the bottle out of the microwave.

''I don't see as how there's ever been a 'mister' anywhere in my name, gal,'' Mose said gruffly. He shook his head. ''You might as well call me Mose, same as everybody else.''

''Okay…Mose,'' she said, turning the bottle up to dribble a couple of drops of milk on the inside of her slender wrist.

When she walked toward Trav, he sucked in a sharp breath. The early morning sunlight beginning to stream in the east window behind her shone right through her thin bathrobe and gown. He swallowed hard. Memories of the way her lithe body had looked, and the sensuous way she moved when they'd been together in Chicago, flooded his mind and caused a definite tightening in the region south of his waistband.

How could he feel any kind of desire for her after what she'd tried to do? Wasn't keeping his child from

KATHIE DENOSKY   47

him enough to douse any lingering feelings he had
for her?

He swallowed hard and averted his eyes to her
lovely face. "What..." he stopped to clear the rust
from his throat "...do I do first?"

"Just make sure to keep it at this angle to prevent
air from getting into the nipple," she said, showing
him the correct way to hold the baby bottle.

Her sweet feminine scent, the softness of her skin
as her hand brushed his and the feel of her breath
feathering over his cheek as she leaned in close to
show him how to feed Autumn had Trav feeling as
if the room temperature had gone up about twenty
degrees. Clearing his throat again, he hoped like hell
he didn't sound like a teenage boy entering puberty
when he asked, "Is that all I need to do?"

Nodding, she draped a cloth over his bare shoulder.
"You two shouldn't have any problems while I'm
upstairs changing. Then, when I come back down, it
should be time to burp her."

He was beginning to wonder if he hadn't bitten off
more than he could chew with this feeding stuff.
"How do I do that?"

"I'll show you when the time comes," she said,
turning to leave the room.

Trav watched her go, the slight sway of her hips
reminding him of just how long it had been since he'd
enjoyed the warmth of a woman. His heart suddenly
sped up, making him feel as if he had a jungle drum
thumping against his rib cage when he realized the

one walking away from him had been the last woman he'd made love to.

Autumn made a slurping noise, drawing Trav's attention back to the product of that lovemaking. Gazing down at the baby that twenty-four hours ago he hadn't even realized existed, Trav wondered how Natalie had looked when she was expecting. Had her pregnancy been easy? Or had she had a difficult time carrying his baby?

He regretted not being there for her. But as he continued to watch his daughter enjoy her morning bottle, he reminded himself that the choice hadn't been left up to him. Natalie had been the one who'd cut him out of being there for both of them.

"How old is that little filly you got there?" Mose asked, pointing to Autumn.

"Two months," Trav said proudly, gazing down at his daughter.

"You got a reason why you didn't marry her momma 'fore she got here?" Mose asked, disapproval written all over his wrinkled face.

"I didn't find out about her until last night," Trav answered, barely able to keep the bitterness he felt from coloring his tone.

He knew better than to tell Mose to mind his own business. As far as the old man was concerned, Trav and Carrie *were* his business, and he was quite adept at giving them the third degree, as well as voicing his opinion whenever he felt they needed it. And that was the case more often than not.

"In my day, when a young buck got a little gal in the family way, he did right by her and put a ring on her finger. Even if it was after the youngun' got here," Mose said, slamming one of the cabinet doors. "I knew your sashayin' around would get you in hot water one of these days."

Rolling his eyes, Trav sighed heavily. He wouldn't bother to argue with Mose, or try to explain that his "sashaying around" had been on business for the TCC. The old codger was on a roll and wouldn't listen until he'd finished saying his piece.

Mose clattered a skillet on top of the stove. "So when are you gonna get that little gal to a preacher and make her your wife?"

Trav glanced up to meet the old man's glare. "I'm not."

"An' jest why ain't you?" Mose retorted. "Way I see it, all you gotta do is take a trip down the aisle to put things right."

"Natalie had an accident," he said, choosing his words carefully. Although the good people of Royal were aware that the TCC assisted people in trouble, most—including Mose—weren't aware of how far the members went in their quest to right the wrongs of the world. "She's had amnesia for the past two months and still can't remember a lot of things."

"Well, she remembered you're that little filly's daddy, didn't she?"

"Yes."

"Then that's all you need to make her your wife."

Mose frowned. "From that accent of hers, I'd say she ain't from around these parts. Where does she hail from, anyway? And why did she wait until the young-un' came along before she looked you up?"

"She's from Chicago," Trav answered, knowing it was useless to try to stop the old man's interrogation. "And I don't know why she didn't let me know she was having my baby."

"Chicago?" Mose scratched his head. "How in the name of Sam Hill did she get all the way down here to Royal? Did she drive by herself with the young-un'?"

"She doesn't remember."

"When did she get here?"

Trav took a deep breath. There was no way around it. He was going to have to fill Mose in, or endure one question after another until the old man dragged everything out of him.

Quickly telling him as much as he knew, Trav added, "That's why Natalie and the baby will be staying with us for a while."

Mose seemed to consider the explanation. "If she got here in November, and you were out of the country till last night, then she came here lookin' for you."

"That's what we figure," Trav said, watching the baby as she continued to drain the bottle. She seemed to have a good, healthy appetite. She'd drank about half of the formula already.

"Then you danged well better do the right thing and marry that little filly's momma," Mose repeated, taking a carton of eggs and a package of bacon from the refrigerator. "How would you feel if some low-down sorry excuse for a sidewinder did the same thing to Bear, then up and left her to face the music?"

Trav's stomach churned at the very thought. "It's not like that."

Mose snorted. "And jest how do you figure it's different? That little gal changin' her clothes upstairs looks to be about the same age as Bear."

"Natalie is a year older than Carrie," Trav said, knowing his argument was as lame as it sounded.

"Well, now, that makes all the difference in the world," Mose said sarcastically. He limped over to stare down at the baby in Trav's arms. His deep scowl softened. "That little girl is right fine lookin', and when she gets older she's gonna need a full-time daddy with a big stick to keep the boys beat back."

That was the closest that Trav had ever heard the old geezer come to paying anyone a compliment—even Carrie-bear. And old Mose thought the sun rose and set on her.

"Don't worry. Every pimple-faced kid who even thinks he wants to smile at her is going to have to get my approval first," Trav said, meaning it.

"How much of the formula has Autumn drunk?" Natalie asked, hurrying back into the room.

Trav looked up and was once again struck by how pretty she was. The first time he'd seen her in the diner in Chicago, he hadn't been able to take his eyes off of her. It appeared she still had that same effect on him. Her violet eyes held a zest for life that fascinated the hell out of him, and her long hair seemed to beg him to tangle his fingers in the silky strands.

He shook his head to dislodge the notion. "I'd say she's downed about half of the bottle, wouldn't you, Mose?"

"'Peers so," the old man said, squinting at the baby bottle with dancing pink bunnies screen-printed along the sides.

"Then it's time to burp her," Natalie said, reaching for Autumn.

"Do you mind if I do it?" Trav asked, wanting to learn all he could about caring for his daughter.

Natalie stared at him for several long seconds. Why was he so interested in finding out about Autumn's care if he meant what he'd said about not taking her to raise by himself?

A chill ran through Natalie. She still didn't trust Travis completely. Had she run from some forgotten source of danger right into the arms of an even worse threat?

"Natalie, are you all right?" Travis asked, frowning.

"I—I'm fine," she finally stammered. "Are you sure you want to try burping her? There are times when it can be pretty messy."

Chuckling, Travis nodded. "I think I can handle anything she throws my way."

"Don't say I didn't warn you." Her pulse sped up

as he continued to look at her. "The cloth I put over your shoulder should catch any spit-up."

His confident look slipped a notch. "Spit-up? You mean she could throw up?"

If she wasn't still worried about Travis trying to take Autumn away from her, Natalie might have laughed at his alarmed expression. "It's not exactly throwing up, but it is something that babies do."

"Does she do it every time she eats?" he asked, suddenly looking concerned. "Have you taken her to a pediatrician about it?"

"No." Natalie surprised even herself by the sharp tone of her voice. But the more she thought about it, the more she knew she didn't want a doctor anywhere near her or Autumn. "It—it's normal for babies to spit up," she said, careful to keep her voice even. "She doesn't need to see a doctor." When she met Travis's questioning gaze, she tried to explain. "I don't like doctors. I can't remember why, but I do know the thought of seeing one makes me extremely nervous."

Mose gave her an awkward pat on the shoulder. "I don't blame you, gal. I don't much like havin' to see a sawbones myself."

As the old man moved off to start breakfast, Travis continued to stare at her. "Do you think your aversion to doctors might have something to do with what happened two months ago?"

"I'm not sure." She nibbled on her lower lip as she tried to think of why she felt the way she did. "I just know that I don't want to have anything to do with doctors of any kind.''

Autumn began to squirm and fuss, indicating that she needed to be burped.

Helping him put the baby to his shoulder, Natalie showed him how to help get rid of the bubble in Autumn's tummy. As she watched Travis gently rub their daughter's tiny back, she again tried hard to recall why she wanted to avoid doctors. The memory felt so close, as if her next thought would clear up the mystery. Then, just as quickly, it was gone.

"How will I know if I've done this right?" He'd no sooner gotten the question out than Autumn let loose a gurgling burp.

"There's your answer," Natalie said, taking the end of the cloth and wiping Autumn's tiny chin.

Travis grimaced. "That sounded really gross."

Natalie couldn't help but laugh. "I tried to warn you."

His smile sent a shiver up her spine. "Yeah, I guess you did."

As she gazed into his hazel eyes, Natalie's heart skipped a beat. She'd fallen in love with him almost eleven months ago, but that was before she'd learned how deceptive he was. She'd do well to remember that.

"I...think I'd better help Mose," she said, suddenly needing to put distance between them.

"What do I do now?" Travis asked, looking bewildered. He picked up the half-empty bottle from the table. "Will she want the rest of this?"

Natalie nodded. "Give her the rest of the formula, then burp her again." Carefully eyeing Fluffy, who lay a few feet from where Mose was frying bacon on the stove, Natalie took a deep breath and started over to help the old gentleman finish preparing breakfast. "After she has a short nap, I'll show you how to give her a bath and change her diaper."

"I'm not sure I'm ready for that," Travis said, sounding doubtful.

"You said you wanted to learn how to help care for her," Natalie said, turning back to face him. "Diaper changes and baths are part of the package."

He stared at her a moment before he gave a short nod. "You're right." Shaking his head, he once again cradled Autumn to his bare chest and held the bottle's nipple to her mouth. "There's more to this baby stuff than meets the eye."

Natalie smiled. Maybe she wouldn't have to worry about Travis wanting to take the baby away from her, after all. Especially once he'd changed a few diapers and had the exhilarating experience of listening to their daughter scream when he gave her a bath.

Four

"Now what do I do?"

Trav stared down at his unhappy daughter lying on a plush towel on the bathroom vanity counter. He'd managed to wrestle her out of her soft pink sleeper, but he didn't have the slightest idea of what to do next.

"Take off her diaper," Natalie answered from the adjoining bedroom. He heard her rummaging around in one of the bags he'd carried up from the SUV after breakfast. "I'll get a clean sleeper and a new diaper."

Once he'd fed Autumn and she'd let loose a burp that any of his old marine buddies would have been proud of, she'd immediately fallen back to sleep. But just when he started feeling pretty confident about his baby-care skills, Natalie had informed him over breakfast that she was going to let him get the full experience of taking care of Autumn, once she woke up.

Now, as he stared down at his daughter, Trav wasn't so sure he was ready for it. Babies didn't come with instruction manuals, and none of the items Natalie had shown him so far had any kind of step-by-step guidelines on them.

"How do you know what to do?" he asked, marveling at how efficient she seemed to be as she laid out everything they would need for Autumn's bath.

"I guess a lot of it's instinct." Shrugging, she moved in to stand beside him. "And there's a certain amount of trial and error thrown in for good measure."

The scent of her herbal shampoo and the warmth of her soft body as she leaned close to unfasten the tapes on Autumn's diaper had Trav swallowing hard and wondering how on earth he was going to keep his hands to himself. Even though he was angry that she'd kept her pregnancy a secret, he still wanted Natalie with a fierceness that made him weak in the knees. And he didn't like it one damn bit.

"Travis, did you hear me?"

"What was that?" He'd been so wrapped up in the way she was making him feel, he'd missed what she'd said.

"I asked if you're paying attention so you'll know what to do," she said patiently.

"Yep. Tear the tapes back and…" he gulped down a groan when Natalie's breast brushed his upper arm "…take the diaper off."

When she instructed him on the proper way to hold the baby while he lowered her into the little plastic bathtub to sponge her off, Trav felt as if his blood pressure went up a good ten points. The sound of Natalie's voice and the feel of her hands on his as she guided him through bathing their daughter was playing hell with his libido. Even Autumn screaming at the top of her little lungs didn't lessen the effect Natalie had on him, and by the time he lifted his squalling little girl from the baby bathtub, perspiration coated his forehead and upper lip.

He wiped the sweat away with the sleeve of his chambray shirt. "What's next?" he asked, hoping Natalie would offer to take over and he could put some much needed distance between them.

Natalie pointed to the plush terry-cloth towel on the marble counter. "Lay her down and pat her dry."

After he'd done as instructed, she handed him a little white container and told him where and how much baby powder to apply to his still-screaming daughter. "Does she cry like this every time you give her a bath?" he asked.

Nodding, Natalie smiled. "You'll get used to it. Now, are you ready for your first diapering lesson?"

"I'm not sure," he said warily. "I don't think I'm very good at this stuff."

Her laughter slid over his senses like a warm summer breeze. "You're the one who wanted to learn how to care for her."

He took a deep breath. "Why do I feel like I'm being set up?"

Natalie just smiled and proceeded to show him how to place the diaper under Autumn, then pull it up between her chubby little legs and secure it at the waist with the side tapes. When he'd struggled through getting the baby all snugged up in a soft yellow sleeper, he felt as if he'd done battle.

Natalie grinned, causing more perspiration to break out on his forehead. "See? That wasn't so difficult, now was it?"

He nodded. "Yes it was." He gazed down at Autumn. "I wish she'd stop crying. It makes me think I'm doing something wrong or that I've hurt her in some way."

"Travis, babies cry for a variety of reasons," Natalie said softly. "It's all they can do to express themselves at that age. Autumn isn't hurt or in pain. Right now, she's letting you know the only way she can that she's angry."

As he stared at Natalie, Trav felt his body begin to respond to the sound of her velvety voice. Turning, he picked up their unhappy daughter to prevent him reaching for Natalie. "I just hate to hear her cry."

"It might help if you start listening to the differences in her crying." Natalie started straightening the bathroom. "Before you know it, you'll learn what message she's trying to get across to you."

He transferred the baby to the cradle of his arm, marveling at how quickly she stopped crying and went to sleep. "Should I put her in bed?"

Nodding, Natalie led the way into the bedroom, where he'd put the portable crib last night. When he placed the baby on the soft flannel sheet, Natalie covered her with a light blanket, picked up a small unit that looked like some kind of listening device, then motioned that they should leave the room.

"Are you sure she'll be all right?" he asked once they stood outside in the hall. He glanced back into the bedroom. "She seems awfully little to be left by herself."

"She'll be fine, Travis." Natalie placed her hand on his arm in a reassuring manner. "I have the baby monitor. If she wakes up I'll hear her."

The warmth of Natalie's touch through the fabric of his shirt sent a sizzling charge up his arm, and before he could stop himself, Trav reached out and took her in an embrace. As he lowered his mouth to hers, he knew he should have his head examined for giving in to the temptation to kiss her. But not even eleven months, or the fact that she'd intended to keep his daughter a secret from him, lessened the effect she had on him. He still wanted her with an intensity that robbed him of breath.

As he tasted her sweetness, her lips parted in a soft sigh and he felt her body relax against his. The small signs of her acceptance urged Trav to deepen the kiss, to explore and tease the sensitive recesses within.

At the first touch of his tongue to hers, his lower body tightened and his heart began to hammer. Bringing his hands up along her sides, he stopped at the swell of her breasts to tease the pebbled tips with the pads of his thumbs. Her moan of pleasure and her arms tightening around his waist as she tried to get closer urged him on, and he couldn't have stopped himself from pressing his rapidly hardening body to her feminine softness if his life depended on it.

A split second later, she pushed against his chest and pulled back. "P-please...stop."

Realizing how fast the kiss had gotten out of hand, Trav dropped his arms and stepped away. He rubbed the back of his neck as he tried to figure out why he'd grabbed her like a teenager with more hormones than good sense. "That shouldn't have happened."

"No...it shouldn't have," she said, sounding breathless. Her eyes warily searched his. "Although I can't remember why I came to Texas, I know for certain that renewing what we shared in Chicago wasn't the reason."

He could have pointed out that she'd been enjoying the kiss as much as he had, but as he silently watched her hurry down the stairs, he decided there was no point in stating the obvious—a lack of passion had never been a problem for them. But she was right about one thing. What they'd had together in Chicago had ended, she wouldn't have come to Texas if not for the trouble she was in.

As Travis considered that she'd headed straight for

Royal when she'd found herself and the baby threatened, a smile tugged at the corners of his mouth, then spread across his face. Natalie might not think he could be trusted any farther than she could pick him up and throw him, but she wouldn't have been trying to find him if she hadn't known he would move heaven and earth to keep her and Autumn from any kind of harm.

Trav checked his watch. It wasn't even noon yet and he'd already had a hell of a New Year. In less than twelve hours he'd discovered the TCC's mystery woman was the same one who'd haunted his dreams for months after his return from Chicago, that he had a two-month-old daughter and whether they liked it or not the passion that had drawn him and Natalie together in the first place was as strong, if not stronger, than it had ever been.

He shook his head. If all that happened in the span of a few hours, he couldn't help but wonder what the rest of the year had in store for him.

Natalie sniffed and wiped the tears from her eyes with her forearm in order to check on what Fluffy was doing. In the five days she'd been staying at Travis's ranch, she'd started to relax around the huge dog, but she still made it a point to know where the animal was and what he was up to. Fortunately, all Fluffy seemed interested in was eating, taking naps and following Mose from one room to another.

Turning her attention back to the onions she was

chopping for the elderly housekeeper to put in a concoction he was planning for dinner, she marveled at the fact that he was the only household help Travis had working for him. She'd always thought someone so wealthy would have staff to do everything for him.

But that didn't seem to be the case. Besides Mose, Travis had only two other people helping him take care of his ranch, and they were cowboys who tended the cattle and horses.

"Mose, where's that meddling brother of mine?" a female voice called a moment before a beautiful red-haired woman with striking hazel eyes came storming into the kitchen. At the sight of Natalie sitting at the table, tears streaming down her cheeks, the woman came to an abrupt halt. Genuine concern replaced her frown. "Are you all right? What's wrong?"

Natalie nodded. "I'm…fine. It's…the onions."

"As much as I paid for 'em, they shouldna been that strong," Mose complained, limping over to awkwardly pat Natalie on the shoulder. "There, there, gal. Why didn't you say somethin' when they started gettin' to you?" he asked gruffly.

"I…told you…I would help," Natalie said, sniffling. "I didn't want to complain…about what you needed me…to do."

"Oh, you poor thing," the woman said, walking straight to the sink. She removed a couple of dish towels from a cabinet drawer, dampened them with cool water and handed one to Natalie. "Be careful not to get your hands anywhere near your eyes, but place this cloth over them. It should help. Mose, take the cutting board over to the counter while I wipe the table,'' she ordered.

"Tarnation, Bear. You're awful dadgummed bossy today," Mose groused. But Natalie noticed that he immediately followed her directive.

The woman he'd called Bear kissed his wrinkled cheek. "I'll continue to be bossy as long as you insist on calling me Bear instead of my name," she said, grinning as she turned to wipe the table's surface with the other cloth. When she'd finished, she turned her attention to Natalie again. "Are your eyes feeling better?"

Natalie nodded. "Thank you…." Her voice trailed off when she realized she'd forgotten Travis's sister's name, and it was clear she didn't like being called Bear.

"I'm sorry. I'm Trav's sister, Carrie," she said, her smile warm and friendly.

"Thank you, Carrie," Natalie said, liking the woman immediately. Rising from her chair at the table, she walked over to wash her hands. "I'm Natalie Perez, a…friend of your brother."

Before either of them could say more, the sound of Autumn waking up from her nap filtered into the room from the baby monitor.

"You have a baby?" Carrie asked, her pretty eyes sparkling with obvious delight. "I love babies."

Natalie nodded, hurrying to get rid of any trace of

the onion before she tended to Autumn. "I just hope she doesn't get too wound up by the time I can get upstairs to see about her."

"Not to worry," Carrie said, turning to leave the room. "I'll go check on her."

Natalie grabbed the soap and started scrubbing her hands. "I'll be right up."

"Which room is she in?" Carrie called from the stairs.

"I think Travis said it's the bedroom you use when you stay over," Natalie answered.

In seconds the sound of Carrie's voice came from the monitor. "Oh, aren't you a cutie!"

When she was satisfied her hands were thoroughly clean, Natalie hurried up the stairs to the room she shared with Autumn. She smiled as she watched Carrie finish fastening the tapes on the new diaper she'd just put on the baby.

"Thank you," Natalie said, meaning it. "She gets extremely angry when she doesn't get a dry diaper right away."

Picking up the infant, Carrie turned to smile at her. "What's her name?"

"Autumn."

"A pretty name for a pretty little girl," Carrie said. "I really like it. It's kind of unusual. Is there a story behind it?"

"I've always like the season," Natalie said. She sucked in a sharp breath as she realized she'd just remembered something else about herself. It was true.

She did like that time of year more than any other, and she knew exactly why she'd named her daughter Autumn. "I love the rich colors and crisp fall air. When I discovered she was due in late October or early November, I knew that's what I wanted to name her."

Natalie watched as Carrie cradled the baby and kissed her round, little cheek. "I would love to have a baby. They're just so sweet." She grinned. "But first, I have to find the right daddy."

"That's important," Natalie said, unsure of what else to say. Should she tell the woman that Autumn was her niece?

"Hey, Carrie-bear. Mose told me that you were looking for me," Travis said from the doorway. He walked over to stand beside his sister. "I see you've met Natalie and our daughter."

Carrie's mouth dropped open. "Your daughter?" She gazed down at the baby for several seconds, then glanced from Travis to Natalie. "You mean this little darling is my niece?"

Grinning, he nodded. "Think you'd like to baby-sit sometime?"

"If you ever call anyone else to watch this little angel, I'm afraid I'll have to hurt you, big brother," Carrie said, smiling down at Autumn. When she looked up again, her expression turned disapproving. "But why didn't you tell me you were going to be a daddy, Trav?"

Travis glanced at Natalie. "I didn't—"

"It's time for Autumn's afternoon bottle," Natalie said, suddenly uncomfortable with the turn the conversation had taken. She stepped forward to take the baby from Carrie. "I'll let Travis explain everything while I feed her."

Trav watched Natalie place a cloth over her shoulder, then without another word carry their daughter out of the room.

"Okay, big brother, it's time for some answers," Carrie said. She pointed to the doorway. "Whatever you're about to tell me clearly makes Natalie uncomfortable."

"Let's go downstairs to my office and I'll fill you in," Trav said, trying to decide how much to tell his sister.

Knowing Carrie-bear, she'd want to go searching for whoever was threatening Natalie and the baby. He chuckled to himself as he followed her downstairs. And God help the thugs if she found them.

His sister was easygoing, fun-loving and as kindhearted as she could be. But she had a protective streak a mile wide when she thought someone was threatening the people she loved. It was one of her most endearing traits, but it was also one of the things about her that bothered him the most. When she got something into her head, it was damn the torpedoes and full speed ahead.

"So what's going on, Trav?" Carrie asked as soon as he shut his office door. "Didn't you know about the baby?"

"No."

"You mean Natalie didn't tell you she was pregnant?" Carrie asked indignantly.

Walking around behind his desk, he sank down in the leather chair, then met his sister's disapproving gaze. She wasn't going to be satisfied until she knew every detail. "I found out about Autumn on New Year's Eve, when I got back from my trip overseas."

Quickly filling Carrie in on what he knew so far about Natalie and the baby, Trav purposely omitted the TCC's role in the investigation. Although there was speculation by most of the townsfolk in Royal about the club's activities, the periodic disappearance of some of its members and the prevention of serious crimes around the globe, the unspoken agreement at the TCC was the less said, the better. Not even close family members knew the full extent of the club's dedication to the pursuit of justice.

"Poor Natalie," Carrie said, sitting down and leaning back in the chair in front of his desk. "She must be scared to death that whoever is chasing them will find her and the baby."

Trav nodded. "That's why I'd appreciate you not saying anything to anyone about them being here."

"My lips are sealed," she exclaimed. "Does Ry know?"

"Yes. And so do some of my other friends."

"You mean the other members of the Cattleman's Club," Carrie said knowingly.

He sighed. Sometimes his little sister was way too

perceptive for her own good. "They were at the party when Natalie recognized me and finally remembered who she is."

"That explains why she showed up in Royal," Carrie said. "But why didn't she tell you about the baby when she found out she was pregnant?"

"Let's just say it was a huge misunderstanding and leave it at that." Trav smiled when Carrie-bear made a face at him. "Natalie and I need time to sort things out between us, not to mention finding out who's after her and the baby, and why."

"That's top priority right now," Carrie agreed. She gave him an understanding smile. "And I know you'll move heaven and earth to keep them safe and find the answers, Trav."

He nodded. "Whoever it is that's chasing them will be sorry when I find him."

"And after you get finished with him, I'll take a turn."

Deciding to change the subject before Carrie went out and started searching for the jerk, he cocked an eyebrow. It was time to start asking a few questions of his own.

"What's this I hear about you wanting to date the new doctor in town?"

"I see you've been talking to Ry," she said, glaring at her brother. "I don't know which one is the bigger busybody when it comes to my love life, you or him."

"We're just concerned for your welfare, Bear."

His sister gave an unladylike snort. "There's a fine line between being concerned and interfering, big brother." He could tell she was gaining a good head of steam when she rose to pace back and forth in front of the desk. "For God's sake, Trav. I'm twenty-four years old, not sixteen. I'm perfectly capable of making my own decisions about who I choose to see socially." She stopped to face him. "And I don't need Ry hanging around intimidating every man I look at for more than two seconds. You can tell him that his watchdog services are no longer needed."

"You're my sister. It's my job to look out for you," Trav said stubbornly. "And did it ever occur to you that Ry is just as concerned for your well-being as I am?"

"Yeah, right." Carrie flopped down in the chair again. "He wouldn't even know I'm alive if you didn't keep asking him to help your efforts at ruining my love life." She glared at him. "Which, by the way, Ry seems to take great joy in doing."

"We're not trying to ruin anything. But have you even met this joker yet?" Trav asked. "Tell me what you know about him. How old is he? Where's he from?"

"His name is Dr. Nathan Beldon. I don't know where he's from, and no, I haven't met him. Yet." Carrie looked Trav square in the eye. "But he has to be more exciting than any of the other men in Royal."

Trav almost laughed out loud. If she only knew the

half of what he and the other TCC members had been involved in, she wouldn't be so eager to label all of them boring.

"Just do me a favor, Carrie-bear."

"What?"

"Don't forget, not everyone is as straightforward and honest as they'd like you to believe," he warned, making a mental note to call Ry and have him keep an even closer watch on Carrie.

"So now you're an expert on human nature?" she asked, raising one perfect auburn eyebrow.

"Nope." Trav shrugged. "I'm a guy. And believe me, I know a whole lot more about what my gender is like than you do."

She laughed as she rose to leave. "You mean there's more to you guys than scratching, spitting and driving around lost for hours on end because you'd rather die than stop to ask for directions?"

He grinned as he followed her out the office door. "Just watch yourself. Okay, brat?"

Turning, she threw her arms around his neck and kissed his cheek. "Don't worry about me so much, Trav. You just get things worked out between you and Natalie. I'm looking forward to having her become my sister-in-law in the not too distant future. That way I'll have Autumn around all the time to love and spoil." She stepped back to give him a questioning look. "Does Natalie have any brothers or sisters?"

"No. Why?"

Carrie-bear beamed. ''I'll be Autumn's favorite aunt and Natalie's favorite sister-in-law.''

Trav frowned as he watched Carrie-bear flounce out the front door. What was it with her and Mose wanting to get him married off?

He glanced toward the kitchen, where he knew Natalie was feeding Autumn a bottle. In the eleven months since his return from Chicago, he hadn't been able to forget the time they'd spent together. But that wasn't the basis for a lifetime commitment.

His heart felt as if it dropped to his boot tops. What the hell was wrong with him? He shouldn't even be contemplating the subject. He'd never given it much thought, but he was pretty sure he wasn't marriage material.

''You're losing it, Whelan,'' he muttered as he headed toward the kitchen.

He'd be the best damn father to Autumn that any little girl could ask for. But marriage—even to the one woman he'd never been able to forget—wasn't in his plans now or in the future.

Five

"Travis?" Natalie stopped just inside his office door to rub her throbbing temples. "Could you watch the baby for an hour while I take a nap?"

"Sure, darlin'." He rose from the chair behind his desk. "Is something wrong?"

She nodded. "I have another headache that I can't seem to get rid of it. I thought if I slept for a little while, it might be gone by the time I wake up."

Walking around the desk, he stopped in front of her, his expression filled with concern. "Have you been having a lot of headaches?"

"I don't think I've ever been prone to them," she said, not really remembering if she had or not. "But I've had one almost every day for the past week."

He put his arm around her shoulders and steered her toward the stairs. "It might be a good idea to see your neurologist if they continue."

"No!" A chill ran up her spine and she began to tremble uncontrollably. "I don't want Dr. McDougal or any other doctor anywhere near me or Autumn."

For a split second, Travis looked surprised by the harsh tone of her voice, then drew her into his strong arms. "It's all right," he said, his voice soothing. He held her close as he gently stroked her hair. "It was just a suggestion. You don't have to go see Dr. McDougal if you don't want to."

Natalie knew she was overreacting, but just the thought of doctors terrorized her as little else could. "I'm...sorry. I can't explain it, but...I have this horrible feeling about doctors. And it seems to be getting worse instead of better."

"Have you always been afraid of them, darlin'?" he asked gently.

"I'm not sure. But I don't think so." She tried to recall her childhood. "I know I liked the pediatrician my parents took me to see when I was a child. But he was more like a grandfather to all of his patients than a doc—"

She stopped short as the whisper of a memory flirted at the corners of her mind. She remembered a handsome man in a white lab coat. His smile was warm and friendly, but his eyes were cold and calculating, as if he had no conscience, no soul. Then, just as quickly as the image appeared, it was gone.

Shivering, Natalie burrowed deeper into Travis's protective embrace. "I'm certain my apprehension was caused by something more recent."

"Do you think it could have something to do with why you came to Royal looking for me?" he asked, brushing his lips across her forehead.

"Maybe." The feel of his light kiss and the warmth of his body surrounding hers made it hard to concentrate on anything but the man holding her to his wide chest. She knew she should move away, but at the moment, she needed the reassurance. "I can't be certain," she finally said, sighing heavily. "It's so frustrating to feel as if I'm close to remembering something important, only to have it slip away."

"I understand, darlin'." He gave her a gentle hug, then, stepping back, cupped her face with his hands. "Let's get you upstairs so you can take that nap. I'll bring Autumn down here with me. She can sit on top of my desk in her baby carrier and keep me company while I work on the ranch books."

"If you need me—"

"I know where to find you." His charming grin made her knees wobble as they climbed the stairs together. "Believe me, if she throws something at me that I can't handle, you'll be the first to know."

Even though her head still hurt, Natalie couldn't help but smile. "You mean if she needs her diaper changed."

Laughing, he put his hand to her back as he guided her into the bedroom. "Yep. I don't mind feeding her, and it doesn't bother me too much anymore when she yells her little head off when I give her a bath. But I'd rather run bucked naked through a patch of prickly pear cactus than change some of those diapers.''

"But I thought marines were able to handle just about anything.'' She caught her breath. "Oh, God. I just remembered that you were in the Marine Corps. You joined after you got out of high school and

your job was to—'' she frowned as she tried to think "—gather some kind of information, right?''

"That's right, darlin','' he said encouragingly. "I was in intelligence. Do you recall anything else?''

"I think you told me you took college courses while you were in the military, then after you were discharged you used the GI Bill to finish your degree.'' She nibbled on her lower lip. "But that can't be right.''

"Why do you say that?''

She shook her head. "Because wealthy people don't go into the military to help finance their education.''

"I haven't always been this well off,'' Trav said, wondering why she sounded so condemning. Deciding it was time to find out, he guided her to the side of the bed, sat down, then pulled her onto his lap. "Natalie, why do you dislike people who have money?''

She nibbled her lower lip again and he knew she was concentrating, trying to remember why she had an intense dislike for the upper class. "Because the rich use people, then cast them aside." Her eyes widened and he could tell she was recalling more things about her life. "My father spent years working for a privately owned company. He helped build the business from the ground up and was only months away from retirement."

"What happened, darlin'?" Trav prompted, trying to help her.

"One day out of the clear blue, the man who owned the Murphy Tool and Dye factory called him in and told my father that he was being let go," she said, staring at the wall as if she watched the events of the past unfolding on a movie screen. "When Dad asked why he was being fired, he was told that it was cheaper to hire someone new to fill his job than to keep him on at top wages, or have to pay benefits he would be qualified to receive if he was allowed to reach retirement."

"Did your dad file fair labor charges against Murphy?" Trav asked, beginning to understand why Natalie felt the way she did.

She paused for several seconds, then shook her head. "He couldn't. Mr. Murphy told Dad what he was doing, and why, in private." Her breath caught. "He even laughed about the vacation home he would buy with what he saved from not having to pay my father his retirement benefits." She closed her eyes for a moment before she could go on. "But the story he told his other employees was entirely different. He swore that my father had made a huge mistake in the purchase of manufacturing materials and that was the reason he was being fired.''

Trav wished he could get this Murphy character in court. He'd have the man so tied up in legal battles the jerk would be more than glad to change his unscrupulous ways.

''Your dad didn't insist on some kind of investigation in order to clear his name?''

''When Dad lost that job, he was so hurt and disillusioned that he…just gave up.'' She impatiently brushed a tear from her porcelain cheek. ''Daddy died less than a year later.''

Trav pulled her close. ''Did Murphy do the same thing to any of his other employees?''

''Yes. But they didn't take it nearly as hard as my dad. I think the reason he lost all interest in living was because he'd thrown himself into his job after my mother passed away. He felt that he had nothing left when Mr. Murphy let him go, and he was suddenly faced with finally having to grieve for his wife, as well as the loss of his job.''

''I'm sure that was hard for him,'' Trav said softly. He wished he could make it right for her and her father. But it was too late. He couldn't bring her father back for her no matter how badly he wanted to.

''The truly sad part of it all is the fact that Daddy probably would have continued working until the day he died and never collected his retirement benefits,'' she said, her voice catching on a sob.

Trav understood why she had her prejudices

against the wealthy, but he had to make her see reason. She condemned him and had even intended to keep Autumn from him because of those prejudices. "Darlin', not everyone with money is as unethical as your dad's former employer."

Pulling from his arms, she stood up. When she turned to gaze down at him, the tears in her eyes just about tore him apart. "You're no different." Rubbing her temples, she shook her head, and he knew she was remembering every detail of the night she'd discovered he was using an alias. "I trusted you, and even after we'd become intimate, you lied to me. You didn't even tell me your real name."

Trav rose from the side of the bed and walked over to her. "Darlin', do you remember any of what I told you that night?"

She took a step back. "I—I'm not sure."

Before she could retreat farther, he put his hands on her shoulders. "Dammit, it's time you stopped trying to convict me before you've heard all the evidence. I explained that I was working on an investigation and that I couldn't tell you who I was because I didn't want to run the risk of blowing my cover."

"But how do I know that wasn't a lie, too?" she asked, clearly unconvinced.

"Natalie, I want you to hear me out. Will you do that?" He held her gaze with his, willing her to say she'd listen. When she nodded, he let out the breath he hadn't realized he'd been holding.

"I'll listen. But how will I know you aren't feeding me another line?" she asked.

"Because everything I'm about to tell you can be verified by Mose, Carrie or any of the Texas Cattleman's Club members," he said, giving her an encouraging smile. "And if that's not enough, I'll show you my bank statements and take you to the county records office."

She stared at him for what seemed an eternity before she finally nodded. "All right."

Deciding to start at the beginning, he took a deep breath. "You were right about me being in the marines. I left for boot camp a few days after I graduated high school. And I did take college classes while I was in the corps, then finished up on the GI Bill once I got out."

"But—"

He put a finger to her lips. "Remember, you promised to let me finish." When she nodded, he went on. "About three months after I got out of boot camp, my parents were killed in a car accident."

"Oh, Travis, I'm so sorry," she said, touching his cheek with her soft hand. "That must have been so hard for you and Carrie."

Trav nodded as he swallowed around the lump clogging his throat. Even though that had been fourteen years ago, it was still hard to talk about. "It was one of the worst times in our lives."

"Did Carrie go to live with relatives until you got out of the marines?" Natalie asked.

He shook his head. "We didn't have any family for her to live with, and I was facing another three and a half years in the military."

"Where did she stay?"

"Fortunately, Ryan Evans's parents took Carrie in. Our dad was the foreman on their ranch, and they loved and cared for her like she was their own daughter."

"I'm so glad she had them," Natalie said.

"Me, too. I don't know what I would have done without their generosity. There was no way I could have afforded to live off base and hire someone to look after her on a private's pay." He gave Natalie a pointed look. "But I did have a plan to secure her future and mine."

"What was that?" she asked, fascinated by the determination she saw in his hazel gaze.

He smiled. "I took the insurance settlement and put it to work. I invested it, along with every spare dime I had, in cattle futures. The market was good and I made a lot of money."

She frowned. "I didn't know there was *that* much money to be made in the agricultural market."

"There is if you know what you're doing," he said. "I was fortunate enough to have a ranching background and an uncanny knack for gauging the market." He shrugged. "Then after my hitch was up with the corps, I invested in real estate and let it build while I finished law school. By the time I passed the bar, I had ensured Carrie's financial future, as well as mine.'' He touched Natalie's cheek with his index finger. ''And, darlin', I didn't have to hurt or step on anyone to get what I have.''

Natalie digested what he'd told her. She had to admit that he'd worked to build his wealth and probably hadn't used anyone to amass what he had. ''But why didn't you explain all that the night I discovered you weren't who you said you were?''

''I was part of a sting operation, and I had to assume a false identity in order to get the information I needed to crack the case.'' Taking her into his arms, he gazed straight at her, and the look in his eyes stole her breath. ''But I tried to be as truthful with you as I could without blowing my cover.'' He smiled. ''Do you know why?''

She shook her head. His closeness, and the feel of his protective arms wrapped so securely around her, robbed her of speech.

''Besides the fact that I hate lying about anything, I wanted you to know the real me.'' He rested his forehead against hers. ''I never said that I didn't have a lot of money. I just didn't tell you that I did. And the only things that I wasn't completely honest about were my name and my real reason for being in Chicago.'' Before she could say anything, he kissed the tip of her nose and stepped back. ''Now, crawl into bed and take your nap.''

''But—''

He put his index finger to her lips. ''We'll talk more about this after you're feeling better.''

Natalie started to tell him that her head no longer hurt, but as she watched Travis strap Autumn into the carrier, she decided she did need time to come to terms with what he'd told her. Had she been judgmental, jumping to the wrong conclusions about him?

"Sweet dreams, darlin'," he said, kissing her cheek. "I'll come up and wake you before supper."

Long after Travis had left her alone, Natalie lay awake mulling over what he'd told her. It was true that the subject of his wealth hadn't come up until the night he'd inadvertently left his wallet at her apartment. And from everything she'd heard about the Texas Cattleman's Club from Tara Andover and Marissa Sorrenson, the members were rumored to be modern-day white knights, using their money and positions to make the world a safer place. The women had told her that it wasn't at all unusual for one or two of the men to disappear for weeks or months, only to have them turn up about the same time the news reported an unknown source had aided authorities in thwarting a crime, or helped bring a criminal to justice.

Had Travis been on a mission for the TCC while he was in Chicago?

The more she thought about it, the more it made sense. He said he'd been using an alias to investigate a sting operation. And she couldn't think of any other reason why a prosecuting attorney from southwest Texas would be working undercover in Chicago.

Yawning, she turned to her side. Seeing Travis in

a new light after all these months was going to take some getting used to.

But as she drifted off to sleep, Natalie dreamed of a white knight righting all the wrongs of the world. And he looked suspiciously like Travis Whelan.

"Billy, go on down to the south pasture and help Juan round up those last two mares," Travis said, pushing his wide-brimmed, black Resistol back with his thumb. "Mose should be calling us to eat pretty soon."

"Will do, boss." The lanky nineteen-year-old dusted his hands off on the seat of his jeans. "I hope Mose made plenty of sandwiches. I think I'm hungry enough to eat a full-size elephant."

Trav laughed as he leaned on the pitchfork he'd been using. "Do you ever get filled up?"

The boy shook his head, his freckled face splitting into a wide grin. "Not very often. Mom says feeding me is like trying to fill a bottomless pit."

"I think she's right," Trav said, grinning as he started forking straw into the stall in front of him.

"Travis?"

Glancing up at the sound of Natalie's voice, Trav frowned. In the week and a half since he'd brought her and the baby to the Flying W, she hadn't ventured outside of the house.

He stabbed the pitchfork into the pile of straw, then walked over to where she stood looking around the inside of the barn. "Is something wrong, darlin'?"

She shook her head. "No. Mose wanted me to come out here to tell you and your men that lunch is ready."

"Afternoon, ma'am," Billy said, nodding as he jogged out of the barn. "I'll go get Juan and be back in a jiffy, boss."

"He seems to be in a hurry," she said, smiling as she stared after the boy.

Trav shrugged. "Billy always moves fast when food is involved."

Frowning, he glanced over at the phone on the far wall of the barn. What was Mose up to this time? Why hadn't the old geezer called him and his two ranch hands to come up to the house?

He pulled his work gloves off and tucked them in the hip pocket of his jeans. "Who's watching Autumn?"

"Carrie."

"I should have known." Unless Trav missed his guess, he'd be seeing a lot more of his sister now that Natalie and the baby were here, which was fine with him. It would make keeping an eye on her a lot easier.

"She stopped by to bring a couple of books she thought I might like to read," Natalie said, wandering over to gaze into Shady Lady's stall. "But I think it was just an excuse to see the baby." When the friendly sorrel mare poked her head over the side of the half door, Natalie smiled. "Oh, aren't you pretty."

"Do you like horses?" he asked, walking over to rub Lady's broad forehead.

Natalie tilted her head to the side, and he could see she was concentrating hard in her effort to remember. "Yes, I think so." She frowned. "It seems odd that a horse doesn't intimidate me, but large dogs…" She sucked in a sharp breath. "I remember why I'm frightened by large dogs."

"Why's that, darlin'?"

Since that headache a few days ago, she had been remembering bits and pieces about her past, but as of yet, she still couldn't recall who was after her and Autumn, or why. He had a feeling it wouldn't be long before she remembered that, as well.

"When I was thirteen, our neighbor's German shepherd dug its way under their fence and bit me," she said, absently rubbing her forearm.

Trav wrapped his arm around her shoulders. "How bad was the bite?"

"I had on a heavy winter coat that protected me from any serious damage, but I remember having an ugly bruise where his jaws clamped down on my arm." She shook her head. "It's really frustrating to remember stupid things like that, but not know what happened two and a half months ago."

He kissed the top of her head. "Give it a little more time, darlin'. You're recalling something new every day now."

"I suppose you're right." She rubbed Lady's soft muzzle. "How many horses do you own?"

"I have twenty right now, but in a couple of weeks I should have five more." He smiled and jerked his thumb over his shoulder toward the stall he'd been preparing. "By the end of the month, Billy and Juan will think they're working in a maternity ward."

Trav watched her eyes widen a moment before she covered her mouth with her hand.

"Natalie?"

"I think I worked in a birthing clinic," she said incredulously.

"You worked in a diner when we met, darlin'," he gently reminded her.

She nodded. "But Mr. Craddock…" She stopped as if to consider what she was saying. "Yes, I'm certain that was his name. He fired me when he found out I was pregnant. He told me that most of the customers knew I wasn't married, and that it wouldn't look right to have an unwed mother waiting tables."

"Whether a woman is married or not, it's illegal to fire her just because she's pregnant." Trav couldn't believe how some employers got away with ignoring the fair labor laws. If he ever got any of them in court, he'd turn them every way but loose and have them more than willing to abide by the Fair Labor Standards Act. "How did you get the job at the clinic?"

"I'm…not sure, but I'm certain it was a birthing clinic." Frowning, she shook her head in obvious confusion. "But why would I work for doctors when I don't want to be anywhere near one?"

"I don't know, darlin'."

He didn't want to upset her or say anything that would stop her recollection of what had happened, but he had a feeling there was a significant connection between her working at the clinic and her recent fear of doctors. He also felt like the biggest jerk the good Lord ever blessed with the ability to walk on two legs for not contacting her once his mission in Chicago had ended.

But the night she'd discovered his identity and demanded that he leave her apartment, he'd told himself he was relieved that their month-long romance was over. The attraction that had drawn them together had developed into a relationship far too fast for his peace of mind.

Now, after getting to know her better, and in light of their having a child together, he should have his ass kicked for giving up so easily. Her lack of trust and intense dislike for anyone with money was well-founded, and he'd only reinforced her beliefs when he'd walked away without a backward glance.

But the main reason he felt lower than pond scum was due to the fact that she'd obviously had to struggle to make a way for herself after she'd gotten pregnant. And something told him that because he had been out of the picture, she'd been forced to accept work that had possibly ended up endangering her and Autumn.

"Do you remember the name of the clinic?" If she did, it might be a place for the TCC to start their investigation.

She paused for a moment, then shook her head. "That's it," she said, her voice filled with disappointment. "I can't remember anything else."

"It's okay, darlin'," he said, pulling her to him. "You've already remembered a lot of things, and I'm betting the rest will come back very shortly."

"I hope so," she said, laying her head against his shoulder.

They stood in silence for several long moments before he finally asked what had been gnawing at him since finding out Autumn was his daughter. "Natalie?"

"Hmm."

He should have his head examined for pushing, but he needed to know. "Did you keep your pregnancy a secret because I have money?"

She drew back to look up at him, then nodded. "Yes."

Anger began to burn at his gut, but he tamped it down. He had a feeling he already knew what her answer would be, but he needed to know for sure. "Why would my having a couple of million dollars matter? Most women would have tried to take me to the cleaners and get as much in child support as the law would allow."

The wariness he'd seen in her eyes the morning after he'd brought her and Autumn to the Flying W was back. "I was afraid if you knew, you would—" she closed her eyes as if she couldn't bear what she was about to say ''—try to take Autumn away from me.''

''What gave you the idea I'd want to do something like that?'' he asked, unable to keep an edge from his voice. ''You should have known me better than that.''

''I discovered you weren't the man I thought I knew,'' she replied defensively.

''But I explained—''

''I understand now why you couldn't tell me your real name or your purpose for being in Chicago,'' she interrupted. ''But at the time, all I knew was that you hadn't been honest. The man I thought you were wouldn't have tried to take my baby from me. But you turned out to be someone else entirely.'' She took a deep breath as if she needed courage to put her fear into words. ''And what chance would I have in a custody battle against someone with your legal background and wealth?''

The last traces of his anger dissipated like mist on a summer breeze. Given her past experience with her father's boss, and disillusioned by the discovery that he was a wealthy lawyer instead of a cowboy from southwest Texas, Trav was beginning to understand what had driven her to make the choices she had. His leaving without putting up so much as a token fight for what they'd shared together hadn't exactly encouraged her to have faith in him, either.

''Do you still think I'd try to gain sole custody of Autumn, darlin'?''

She nibbled her lower lip. ''I don't think you

would.'' She stared at him a moment, then touching his face with her soft palm, added, ''But I do know you'd never let anyone else take her from me.''

Her unwavering faith that he would keep their daughter safe sent a shaft of longing straight through him, and Trav made a vow right then and there that if it killed him, he'd never let her down again. And a good start at making things right for her now would be to let the other TCC members in on what she'd remembered. They needed to know about her working at the clinic and the panic she experienced whenever anyone mentioned her or Autumn seeing a doctor. Some of the guys could check it out and possibly turn up a lead that way.

''We'd better get up to the house,'' he finally murmured. ''Mose will skin me alive if we're not there to eat when he thinks we should be.''

''You have a very unique relationship with him, don't you?'' she asked.

''Not really.'' Trav kissed the top of her head. ''I pay him each month, and in return he cooks, cleans and tries to run my life.''

''From what I've seen, he's pretty good at his job,'' she said, laughing softly.

Chuckling, Trav nodded and guided her toward the barn's double doors. ''If he got any better at it, I doubt I'd have any say around this place at all.''

Natalie smiled. In the past couple of weeks, she'd seen Travis in a variety of situations, and he was nothing like she'd always believed millionaires to be. Instead of arrogantly issuing orders to his ranch hands, and treating them as if they were beneath him, more times than not he asked if they minded doing whatever he wanted done. And he wasn't above working alongside the two boys, doing the dirtiest of tasks.

But even more amazing than his attitude toward his ranch hands was the way he treated Mose. She could tell Travis genuinely cared for the old gentleman, and it wasn't at all unusual for Mose to tell Travis what he thought, or what Travis should or shouldn't do in any given situation. Travis always listened, and at times ended up taking his advice.

Unfortunately, circumstances were different for them now than they'd been in Chicago. Aside from the fact that she and Trav had been apart for the better part of a year, he was back in his element and no longer in need of her company to fill the lonely hours of being in an unfamiliar city. And someone was threatening her and the baby for a reason Natalie couldn't for the life of her remember.

A strange sadness filled her as they crossed the inner courtyard and walked toward the kitchen door. They might be together once again, but in some respects they were further apart than they'd ever been.

Six

Once he'd parked his SUV in the Texas Cattleman's Club parking lot, Trav checked his watch. He was a few minutes late for the meeting he'd called, but that couldn't be helped. Natalie had another headache and he'd been taking care of the baby. And as committed as he'd always been to the club and their motto of Leadership, Justice and Peace, Natalie and Autumn came first right now.

Entering the same clubhouse that Henry ''Tex'' Langley had built back in 1910 when he'd founded the TCC, Trav walked through the elegant foyer. He took little notice of the oil paintings of past members hanging on the walnut paneled walls, or the rich elegance surrounding him as he crossed the lounge.

He nodded a greeting to a couple of older members seated in leather armchairs beneath one of the many mounted big game animals gracing the salon's walls. A crystal brandy decanter and two half-filled, matching tumblers sat on the small, ornate table between them. He'd bet the two old men were drinking a toast to some of the missions they'd conducted in their younger days.

Reaching a door on the far side of the lounge, Travis opened it and stepped inside the smaller room that had been reserved for their meeting. David Sorrenson, Ry, Alex Kent, the sheik and Clint Andover looked up expectantly.

"What's up, Trav?" Ry asked.

"Sorry I'm late. I had to give the baby a bath." He noticed amused grins appearing on his friends' faces. "What?"

"You're really getting into this father thing, aren't you?" Alex asked, smiling widely.

Trav shrugged as he took his seat in one of the maroon leather chairs that had been arranged in a semicircle for their meeting. "Don't knock it until you've tried it, Kent."

Alex held up both hands. "Not me. I'm too set in my ways for that kind of stuff."

"Did Jane—I mean, Natalie—remember something relevant about the case?" Clint Andover asked. He'd just returned from honeymooning in Europe, and Trav could honestly say he'd never seen the man look more relaxed or happy.

Before he could answer, or congratulate Clint on his recent marriage, a waiter quietly appeared. "Good afternoon, sir. May I get your usual drink, or would you like something stronger today?"

Trav shook his head. "A beer would be fine, Jimmy. Thanks." Once the formally dressed waiter had left the room as quietly as he'd appeared, Trav met his friends' questioning gazes. "Natalie remembered that she worked at a birthing clinic just prior to having the baby. But she's terrified of doctors and can't stand the thought of her or the baby being anywhere near one."

"Does she remember the name of the clinic or the doctor she worked for?" David Sorrenson asked, sitting forward.

"Not yet." When Jimmy opened the door on the other side of the pool table, then crossed the room to serve him the beer he'd requested, Trav waited until the man silently left the room again before he continued. "And she still doesn't have a clue why she had five hundred thousand dollars in Autumn's diaper bag."

"It will all come back to her soon," Darin predicted over the rim of his coffee cup.

"That's what I figure," Trav said, taking a drink of his beer.

Once they'd discussed the details Natalie had remembered, the possibilities of what they might have to do with the clinic and how to proceed with the investigation, Clint rose to his feet. "I think our best bet will be to keep our eyes open for any more activity from the thugs who torched Tara's house, and wait for Natalie to remember the name of that clinic.''

"I agree," David said, standing to follow Clint to the door leading into the lounge. ''Once we have that, we can investigate the clinic's owner.''

"Hey, where are you two going?" Ry asked, his eyes filled with amusement.

Clint gave him a lopsided grin. ''I'm a newlywed, hotshot. Where do you think I'm going?''

David laughed. ''I'm headed home to my wife, too. She's a hell of a lot nicer to look at than you guys.''

"I think I'll head on out to see what's happening in the lounge," Alex said, joining the pair. ''Maybe I can get a card game going with some of the older guys.''

"If you need my assistance, I will be at my cousin's ranch," Darin said, following Alex through the door.

When Ry rose to leave, Trav stopped him. ''Do you have a couple of minutes?''

"Sure." His friend looked a little apprehensive. ''You're going to ask me to continue to baby-sit Carrie-bear, aren't you?''

"I won't tell her that you refer to keeping an eye out for her as baby-sitting," Trav said, grinning. ''It could be hazardous to your health if she found out.''

"Hell, I'm already working on an ulcer just trying to keep up with her," Ry said, rubbing his flat stomach. "She's started trying to give me the slip whenever I see her out somewhere now."

"Has she even met this Beldon character yet?" Trav asked.

Ry shook his head. "Not that I know of. He sticks to himself when he's not at the hospital." He smiled wryly. "And it's driving Carrie-bear nuts. All she really knows about him is that he's tall, dark and single." Ry laughed. "Hell, even I've got those qualifications, if that's what she's looking for."

Trav detected a tinge of resentment in Ry's tone, and he couldn't help but wonder why. Could Ry be seeing Carrie as more than his best friend's kid sister?

"If you could keep an eye on her until I get this thing resolved with Natalie and the baby, I'd really appreciate it," Trav said, knowing that his friend would put up a token protest, then agree.

"Before this is over with, Carrie-bear's going to skin both of us alive, then nail our sorry hides to the barn door," Ry said, shaking his head.

"You know I wouldn't ask if I didn't already have my hands full with this threat to Natalie and the baby," Trav said earnestly. Deciding to play his trump card, he added, "I just have a bad feeling about this joker she's set her sights on."

It wasn't a lie. Beldon's reluctance to socialize bothered Trav. A lot. It was abnormal for a doctor wanting to set up a new practice in a community-minded town like Royal not to get out and mingle with the residents. It gave the impression that the man thought he was better than the people he would be treating, or that he had something to hide.

"Aw, hell, Trav. You know you can count on me," Ry said, just as he'd expected. "But I'm sending you the bill when I end up seeing a doctor for the ulcer I'm going to get."

Trav laughed as he opened the door and they crossed the lounge on their way out of the clubhouse. "Stop by the drugstore on your way out of town and buy a roll of extra-strength antacid tablets."

"Mose, do you know where Travis is?" Natalie asked, tensing when Fluffy rose from where he lay at the old man's feet to amble over to her.

"After he got back from his meetin' in town, he went down to the barn to check on Shady Lady," Mose answered, jerking his thumb toward the door. "He said she's showin' signs of droppin' her colt sometime within the next day or two."

It was hard to concentrate on what the old gentleman was saying and still keep her eyes on Fluffy. When the dog gazed up at her with soulful eyes, then flopped down at her feet, she let out a relieved breath. Although she didn't fear the big animal as much as she had when she'd first arrived at Travis's ranch two weeks ago, he still made her nervous.

"Well, I'll be danged," Mose said, his normal frown replaced by a rare grin. "Looks like Fluff's made up his mind about you."

"What do you mean?" she asked, glancing down

at the dog and hoping that he hadn't decided she'd be tasty.

"He don't lay down by just anybody," Mose said, chuckling. "Only family gets the privilege of trippin' over him every time we turn around."

Natalie had a hard time swallowing around the lump that formed in her throat. It was completely ridiculous to be so emotional, but it had been quite awhile since anyone considered her part of their family, even a dog.

She tentatively reached down to pat Fluffy's head. Her heart came up in her throat when he raised up and licked her entire hand with one swipe of his tongue. To her amazement, he didn't try to bite her. He just lay at her feet, his big tail thumping the tile like a thick, heavy piece of rope.

"See?" Mose said, limping over to pat her on the shoulder. "He just sealed the deal with a kiss. You're one of his people now."

"One of his people?" she asked, laughing.

"With a mastiff, he claims you, and that's the way it is. Sorta like him ownin' you, instead of you ownin' him."

She reached down to pet Fluffy again, and was rewarded with another slurp of his tongue on her hand. "He does seem to like me. Either that or he's tasting me to see if I'd make a good snack."

Still a bit uncertain about Fluffy's intentions, she jumped when two strong arms circled her waist from behind to draw her back against a solid male chest.

"Oh, dear heavens!" Her heart skipped a beat and she wasn't sure if it was due to being frightened, or from the nearness of the man holding her to him. "You scared the daylights out of me, Travis."

"I'm sorry, darlin'." His deep baritone sent a shiver streaking up her spine, and the feel of his solid maleness pressed to her back from shoulders to knees caused her stomach to do a back flip.

"I—I've been looking for you," she said, wondering if that throaty female voice was actually hers.

"Now that you've found me, what are you going to do with me?" he teased.

Natalie blushed all the way to the roots of her hair when she noticed Mose's ear-to-ear grin. "I wanted to tell you that I remembered something else about the birthing clinic."

"What is it?" he asked, turning her in his arms to face him.

"It's probably nothing, but every time I think about the clinic, I not only feel panic, I also feel very sad," she said, frowning. "I don't know why, but I know it wasn't a happy place, like you'd think a birthing clinic would be. There was a lot of sorrow."

Natalie wasn't sure if the sadness she felt about the clinic was significant to the danger she and Autumn were in, or if she was remembering something specific that had happened while she worked there. But her fear, anxiety and now the sadness all seemed to revolve around doctors and that clinic. There had to be some kind of connection. She just wished she remembered what it was.

"Anything else?" Travis asked quietly. She could tell he was trying to help her without pushing.

Frowning, she shook her head. "It feels like my next thought will clear up everything, but try as I might, it just won't come."

"It sounds like you're trying too hard to remember, darlin'." He kissed the tip of her nose. "What do you say we relax this evening, forget about everything and do something fun?"

"Wh-what did you have in mind?" The smile he gave her warmed her all the way to her soul, and at the moment, she couldn't think of anything but the way he was looking at her.

"Do you remember how we used to eat popcorn and veg out on the couch at your apartment while we watched old movies?"

Swallowing hard, she nodded. That was one of the first memories to come back to her when she'd seen him at David and Marissa's party. Travis and she had spent almost every evening at her apartment watching movies, and it had always led to them making love and him spending the rest of the night holding her while they slept.

"Yes, I remember everything up to being fired at the diner," she said, finding it hard to draw a breath. "I just can't recall who I worked for after that, the name of the clinic or what happened between going to work there and waking up in the hospital here."

"Forget about it for tonight." He grinned. "What do you say we stuff ourselves with popcorn and watch your favorite movie after Autumn goes to sleep?"

She smiled. "You actually remember which one that is?"

Nodding, he leaned down to whisper in her ear. "I've got *It Happened One Night* with Clark Gable and Claudette Colbert on DVD."

Natalie's heart skipped a beat. He had remembered that she loved the classic romantic comedy. But more than that, she could tell he recalled it was the movie they'd watched the first night they'd made love.

Her pulse quickened and she swallowed hard. "I, um, I'm not sure that's a good choice."

"Sure it is. It's a feel-good movie, and perfect for a first date." Pressing a quick kiss to her lips, he stepped back. "I'll meet you in the family room at nine."

"What if I decide I'd rather stay in my room and read, or go to sleep early?" she asked, not sure she liked him calling it a date.

Travis gave her a grin that turned her insides to warm pudding. "I'll just have to come upstairs and get you, darlin'."

Seated beside Natalie on the overstuffed couch in the family room, Trav switched off the lamp on the end table, grabbed the remote control, then propped his feet on the coffee table. "Ready, darlin'?"

"Why did you turn the lights off?" she asked, clearly startled.

"You always said you like them off because it's more like being in a movie theater." He pushed a button to start the DVD player, then placed the remote control on the end table and reached into the bowl she clutched as if it was some kind of lifeline. "I had Mose leave the butter off the popcorn because I know you don't like it."

She gazed at him a moment before asking, "You remembered all those things about me?"

He nodded. "Darlin', I remember everything about our time together in Chicago." Stretching his arm out along the back of the couch behind her head, he tangled his fingers in the silky, golden-brown strands of her hair. "You don't like coffee, but you love hot tea with honey and lemon. Your favorite color is any shade of pink. You had a goldfish named Romeo when you were in grade school." He leaned close to whisper, "And I also remember you sleep on the right side of the bed and love to cuddle after making love."

Her eyes widened. "Travis, I don't think—"

"Shh, darlin'," he said, placing his finger to her perfect coral lips. "The show is starting."

For the next hour and a half they sat in companionable silence as Clark Gable and Claudette Colbert found themselves in one predicament after another. As the ending credits rolled up the big-screen TV, Trav reached over and turned on the lamp.

"Would you like to watch another old movie?" he

asked, pushing the button on the remote to eject the DVD. "I have several of your favorites."

"I didn't think you liked old movies," she said, turning to face him. "Now that I think about it, I distinctly remember you telling me you preferred action-adventure films."

Smiling, he put his arm around her shoulders and pulled her over to kiss the top of her head. "That was before I met a pretty Chicago waitress who turned me on to the movie classics of the thirties and forties."

He watched her nibble her lower lip a moment before she met his gaze head-on. "Could I ask a question, Travis?"

"Ask me anything you want, darlin'."

"Why did you remember all those things about me and start watching old movies?"

"Because I couldn't forget," he said honestly. He put the remote down, then pulled her onto his lap. "And I started watching old movies because they reminded me of you."

"I...don't know what to say." She looked more than a little shocked by the revelation.

Arranging her long hair over her shoulder, he pressed a kiss to the hollow behind her ear. "Were there things about me that you couldn't forget, Natalie? Times when something would remind you of me and some of the things we'd done together?"

When her gaze locked with his, she nodded. "I thought about you every day. I remembered that you like your iced tea sweet and your steaks medium-well.

Your favorite color is blue, and you sing George Strait songs every morning when you take a shower."

For reasons he couldn't explain, and didn't care to analyze at the moment, Trav felt warmed all the way to the depths of his soul. Hugging her close, he asked, "Do you recall the first movie we watched together?"

"*Arsenic and Old Lace* with Cary Grant," she said, smiling. "It's another one of my all-time favorites."

He grinned. "The second night we watched *Casablanca* and the night after that—"

She leaned back to stare at him. "You remember every movie we watched and the night we watched it?" she asked incredulously.

He chuckled. "Not exactly. But I do recall a lot of them." Lowering his head, he added, "And the movie we just finished watching was the one we saw the first night we made love."

Natalie caught her breath when his mouth brushed hers. "Travis, I don't think this is a good idea."

"Probably not," he said, nibbling kisses from the corner of her mouth to the hollow behind her ear. "But do you want me to stop?"

"No...yes." She tried to draw some much needed air into her lungs. How was she supposed to think when the touch of his lips to her sensitized skin made her heart skip every other beat? "I'm...not sure."

"You want to know what I think?" he asked, his voice low and intimate.

Unable to form words, she barely managed to nod as a wave of heat coursed through her.

"I think you like the way I'm making you feel. You're just not sure you should," he whispered. His warm breath feathering over her ear sent a delicious shiver streaking up her spine. "Isn't that right, darlin'?"

"Y-yes."

"Then leave the decision to me."

Before she could object, his mouth covered hers, and anything she'd been about to say vanished like mist in the wind. The feel of his firm, male lips on hers, the clean, masculine scent of him surrounding her and the knowledge that she was in the arms of the man she'd once loved with all of her heart, sent her good sense right out the window and her will to protest right along with it. She wanted to taste his passion, once again experience the power and strength of his kiss.

Lifting her as if she weighed no more than their tiny daughter, he laid her on the couch, then stretched out beside her and gathered her to him. "This is something else I couldn't forget," he said, brushing his lips over her eyes, her cheeks and the tip of her nose. "You have the softest skin and the sweetest kisses."

When he touched her lips with his fingertip, every nerve in her body tingled to life. "Please..."

His hazel eyes darkened to brown. "What do you want, darlin'?"

"Please...kiss me, Travis," she said, thirsting for the taste of him. "Really kiss me."

She'd no sooner gotten the words out than his mouth fused with hers and her eyes drifted shut. The feel of Travis's lips moving over hers and the delightful teasing of his tongue as he coaxed her to open for him sent heat racing through her veins and caused tiny points of light to sparkle behind her closed eyelids.

Natalie responded without a moment's hesitation, and as he slipped his tongue inside to trace the inner recesses, every inch of her body sizzled. Stroking her with a tenderness that brought tears to her eyes, he slid his hand down to cup her bottom and draw her hips to his. The feel of his insistent arousal nestled intimately at the juncture of her thighs caused the tingling sensations skipping along her nerve endings to turn to tiny jolts of electrified desire, and she couldn't have stopped a moan from escaping if her life depended on it. But the sound did help to penetrate the sensual haze surrounding her, and Natalie wondered what on earth she was doing.

Even though she and Travis had come to an understanding about their parting in Chicago she didn't think it would be wise to pick up their relationship where they'd left off, as if nothing had happened. They had a child to think about now, and Autumn's welfare had to come before anything else. Making love with Travis could very well complicate things further and make working out shared custody more difficult.

Apparently sensing her inner turmoil, he lightened

the kiss, then drew back to take a deep breath. "Darlin', I'm not going to tell you that I don't want you." He chuckled as he pressed his lower body closer to hers. "We'd both know I was lying through my teeth if I did." Bringing his hand up to cup her breast, he traced his thumb over the peak as he captured her gaze with his. "But I can wait. Nothing is going to happen until you're ready for it."

"I…it's not that I don't want…" Her voice trailed off as she tried to gather her scattered thoughts. If she wasn't careful, she'd end up admitting things that she hadn't come to terms with herself.

"I know, darlin'," he said, kissing the tip of her chin. "We need to concentrate on you regaining your memory and ending the danger to you and the baby before anything else." Rising to his feet, he smiled as he held out his hand to help her up. "What do you say we call it a night? Our daughter will be waking up in about six hours for her breakfast. And if there's one thing I've learned in the past two weeks, it's that she isn't long on patience."

"No, she's not," Natalie agreed, accepting his help getting up from the couch. She picked up the baby monitor from the end table.

When they reached the room she shared with the baby, he took the unit from her. "I'll take care of Autumn's breakfast in the morning, darlin'. Have sweet dreams of old movies—" he gave her a kiss that made her knees wobble "—and me."

Seven

An hour later, Trav punched his pillow, turned on his side and pulled the comforter up to just below his chin. His body was still cool from the cold shower he'd taken, but the chilling spray had done little to lessen the desire he had for the woman just across the hall. He wanted Natalie with an intensity that left him feeling light-headed, and he could tell she felt the same way about him.

But he fully understood her hesitancy. She was still trying to regain her memory, get used to the demands of being a new mother, and deal with the unknown danger that had brought her to Royal in the first place. Making love with him now would only add another element to the puzzle of her life, not to mention complicating his.

As he lay beneath the covers, trying to will his body to relax, the sound of Natalie's terrified voice coming through the baby monitor sent a chill snaking up his spine that had nothing whatsoever to do with his icy shower. "*No!* You can't take my baby."

Throwing the comforter back, Trav was on his feet and across the hall in a flash. Without a thought to the fact that he was wearing only a pair of boxer shorts, he opened Natalie's door and rushed over to sit on the edge of the bed.

"It's all right, Natalie," he said, lifting her to hold her trembling body close. He switched on the bedside lamp to help chase away the remnants of the dream. "You had a nightmare."

"Check…to see that Autumn is…still in the crib," she insisted, her voice sounding as if she was on the verge of hysteria.

When he'd done as she requested, he came back to sit down beside her. "The baby is fine, darlin'. She's still sound asleep." Taking Natalie into his arms again, he tried to calm her. "I promise it was just a nightmare. You and the baby are both safe."

"Oh God, Travis…it was so real," she said, clutching him as if he were a lifeline.

Her tears on his shoulder burned like a brand and caused a knot to form deep in the pit of his belly. He hated seeing her this upset, but knowing that he couldn't do anything to lessen Natalie's fear was almost more than he could take.

"I know, darlin'." He ran his hands up and down

her slender back in an effort to soothe her. When he finally felt her begin to relax, he asked, "Do you want to tell me what the dream was about? Sometimes it helps to talk about it."

"I can't remember who was chasing me, but…there were two of them," she said, her voice catching. She leaned back to push the hair away from her face. "I was at the bus station in Amarillo and—" Her eyes widened suddenly and she covered her mouth with both hands in an effort to muffle a startled cry.

"What is it, Natalie?"

She was scaring the living hell out of him. Her body had begun to shake uncontrollably and she was as pale as a ghost. When she continued to stare off into space, Trav could tell she was reliving something terrible.

Cupping her face with his hands, he forced her to look at him. "Talk to me, Natalie. Tell me what's wrong, darlin'."

Her eyes finally focused and the absolute terror he saw in their violet depths just about tore him apart. "My God, Travis. It wasn't…a dream. It…actually happened."

He took a deep breath in an effort to control the fury building in his gut. He needed to stay calm for Natalie's sake. But what he really wanted to do was find whoever had done this to her and rip the bastard apart with his bare hands.

"Start at the beginning, darlin'." He took her shaking hands in his. "What's the first thing you remember about being in the Amarillo bus station?"

"I was holding Autumn and I knew someone was trying to take her from me." She stopped to draw a deep breath. "I'd made it to a row of buses and I was trying desperately to reach the one I needed to get on when I was hit from behind. Then someone moved in from the side and tried to pull Autumn out of my arms." Natalie's grip tightened on his hands. "I don't know who they were, but there were two of them." Her voice shaky, she added, "I think the one trying to take Autumn away from me was a woman."

"Are you sure?" he asked, knowing it could be a significant lead for the TCC to check out.

"Yes, I'm certain," she said, nodding.

"Do you remember anything else, darlin'?" he asked, hoping she'd recall something specific. It could be a scar, the distinct sound of a voice—anything that might give them a lead to go on.

She shook her head. "No. The only thing I'm sure about is that I was hit on the head from behind, while the woman tried to take Autumn."

Trav frowned. "But David, Clint and Alex said your forehead was bleeding when you stumbled into the diner that night."

Reaching up to touch her head, she nodded. "I remember being knocked against the side of a bus when I was hit, and I think I banged my head."

"Do you remember how you got away from them?"

She shook her head. "No."

"Do you recall any other passengers? Someone who witnessed the assault? Maybe the driver saw something."

"I'm not sure," she said, frowning. "I remember the bus I fell against was empty and there were a couple of buses between it and the one I needed to get on." Tears filled her eyes. "Oh, Travis, why would someone do that? Why would they try to take my baby from me?"

Pulling her back into his arms, he held her tightly. "I don't know, darlin'." He kissed her forehead. "But you and Autumn are safe now. I promise you that as long as I have breath left in my body, no one will hurt either one of you."

When he started to let her go and get up, she clutched at his biceps. "I...don't want to be alone." Gazing at him with pleading eyes, she added, "Please, hold me a little while longer."

At that moment, if she'd asked for the moon he'd have found a way to get it for her. "I'm not going anywhere, darlin'."

Laying her back against the pillows, he stretched out beside her and pulled the covers up over them. When he gathered her to him, she rested her head on his shoulder and pressed herself to his side.

"I know I'm being silly but..." she shivered "...I can't shake the horrible feeling of having someone try to steal Autumn."

Trav scrunched his eyes shut and tried to concentrate on what she'd said, instead of the way she felt snuggled against him. With her warm, feminine form touching every inch of his right side and her soft hand resting on his bare chest, he was reminded of just how long it had been since he'd held her like this.

"Don't think about what almost happened, darlin'," he finally managed to murmur.

"I'll try," she said, sounding sleepy.

The feel of every feminine peak and valley through her thin, cotton nightshirt was enough to send his blood pressure up at least fifty points. And when her soft sigh feathered across his nipple, Trav was sure it spiked into stroke range. Deciding he was caught somewhere between heaven and hell, he gritted his teeth to keep from groaning out loud.

He wanted her with every fiber of his being, but the timing couldn't be worse. Natalie was trusting him to lend her his strength, not offer her his lust.

When he realized she'd gone to sleep, he let out the breath he hadn't known he'd been holding, and tried to relax. He needed to concentrate on helping her regain the rest of her memory and on bringing the ones chasing her to justice. Making a mental note to let the other TCC members in on the latest development, Trav pressed a kiss to her forehead.

Now that he'd been given a second chance with Natalie, he'd walk through hell before he let anyone take her or their daughter away from him.

Natalie went perfectly still at the feel of a man's arm draped over her, holding her securely to his seminude body. But as she remembered the nightmare and her request that Travis stay with her, her heart swelled with emotion. He'd kept his word and held her close throughout the rest of the night.

Turning, she studied his handsome face. He was such a kind, considerate man, and since coming to stay with him on the Flying W, she'd discovered that he had a strength of character that most men only hoped to possess. But in the process of learning more about Travis, she'd also discovered something about herself.

She took a deep breath. It was past time that she admitted she'd been a stubborn, prejudiced fool. For years, she'd believed that everyone with money was as ruthless and uncaring as her father's boss. But Travis had proved her wrong, time and again.

When he first discovered that Autumn was his child, Natalie knew he'd been hurt and angry with her for keeping her pregnancy a secret. But instead of condemning her, as he had every right to do, he'd set his own feelings aside, going out of his way to reassure her that he would keep her and the baby safe from all harm. He'd even taken a leave from his job in order to spend time with her and the baby. She lightly touched his cheek with her fingertips. And he'd done everything he possibly could to help her regain her memory.

"Morning, darlin'," he said, smiling at her. "Like what you see?"

Natalie caught her breath. "How long have you been awake?"

"Since you turned over to face me." He nuzzled the neckline of her nightshirt out of the way to kiss her shoulder.

"I, um, didn't know whether I should wake you," she said, cringing at the lame excuse. "I thought I'd let you sleep when Autumn wakes up for her bottle."

His grin sent a wave of heat coursing through her veins. "I've already given her a bottle, changed her diaper and she's been asleep..." he checked his watch "...for the past half hour."

Natalie frowned. "How did I manage to sleep through all that?"

Pulling her to him, he brushed her lips with his. "You had a bad scare last night, and I wanted you to get some rest," he said quietly. "As soon as I heard her first whimper, I got up to see about her."

He was going to be an amazing father, and Natalie felt guilty for even thinking about keeping Autumn from him. "Travis, I...I'm so sorry."

Leaning back, he looked surprised. "What for, darlin'?"

"I should have told you when I found out I was pregnant."

Travis stared at her for several seconds before he nodded. "I would have been there with you every step of the way."

She swallowed. "I know that now. But at the time, I still believed—"

"The worst of me." His charming grin softened the blunt assessment. But as he tucked her hair behind her ear, his expression turned serious. "What was it like for you during your pregnancy, darlin'? Did everything go smoothly, or did you have problems?"

"I was sick every morning for the first couple of months." She grimaced. "It wasn't pretty. But after that I felt good."

"I should have been with you." He shook his head as he placed his hand on her stomach. "I could kick myself for not contacting you after the case I was working on came to an end."

His touch sent a wave of longing straight to her core. "I doubt that it would have done any good. I was still pretty hurt and disillusioned with you."

"Did you ever intend to let me know that you'd had my baby, Natalie?" he asked softly.

She took a deep breath as she considered how to answer his question. "I'd like to think that I would have eventually."

"I'd like to think that you would have, too," he said, lifting the hem of her nightshirt. He slowly slid his hand up her abdomen to the underside of her breast. "Were you upset when you found out that I'd gotten you pregnant, darlin'?"

Hesitating, she shook her head. "After the initial shock wore off, I started looking forward to having a baby." Her heart skipped a beat when his hand cupped her breast, and she found it extremely hard to draw a breath. She should stop him. But heaven help her, she wanted Travis's touch, wanted to feel his hands caressing her body. "I knew…I'd have someone to love again…who I hoped would…love me in return."

His gaze held her captive as he leaned forward. "You have no idea how much it means to me, knowing that you wanted to have our baby, Natalie."

When he covered her mouth with his, his lips moved over hers with such care it brought tears to her eyes. A delicious tingling sensation streaked through her as he urged her to open for him. And when his tongue dipped inside to stroke hers, her eyes drifted shut and she gave herself up to the exquisite heat flowing through her veins.

Bringing her arms up, she encircled his shoulders and held him to her. She loved the way Travis kissed. Whether soft and gentle or insistent and passionate, he always created an excitement within her that she'd never experienced with any other man.

As he continued his sensual assault on her mouth, he caressed her breast with his callused palm, chafing the pebbled tip with the pad of his thumb. Natalie moaned from the intense impulses that seemed to arrow straight to her womb.

He raised his mouth from hers to scatter tiny kisses down the column of her neck to the rapidly beating pulse at the base of her throat. "Do you like the way that feels, darlin?"

Her eyes still closed, she nodded. "Y-yes."

"Look at me, Natalie." When she did, the hunger

she saw in his hazel gaze took her breath away. "I want to love you, darlin'. But if that's not what you want, tell me now."

As she stared up at his handsome face, she knew making love with him was the last complication she needed to add to her enigmatic life. But whether she should or not, Natalie didn't have the will to resist. She wanted to once again know the tenderness of his love, to feel his body locked with hers in the ultimate embrace a man and woman could share.

"That's what I want, too," she said as she threaded her fingers through the hair at the nape of his neck. "Make love to me, Travis."

Natalie's heart pounded like a jungle drum when Travis gave her a slow smile filled with promise, then shifted closer. The feel of his strong arousal pressed against her thigh, and the look of hungry desire in his hazel gaze, sent a shiver of need straight through her.

"Darlin', I'm going to do my best to make this last," he said, brushing her lips with his. "But it's been so damn long, and I want you more than I've ever wanted anything in my life."

His heated gaze held her captive as he reached down to slide his hands along her sides, pushing her nightshirt up and over her head. Without a second thought, she raised her arms to help him, and in no time he had the garment tossed to the floor.

Leaning down, he kissed the slopes of her breasts. "You're so beautiful," he murmured as his lips skimmed one taut nipple. "So perfect."

When he took the tight tip into his mouth, her breath caught and she had to bite her lower lip to keep from moaning as a delicious tension began to thread through every part of her. And as his tongue traced lazy circles around the hardened peak, the ribbons of desire wove into a coil of heated need deep in the most feminine part of her.

Unable to stop herself, she whispered his name as she held him to her.

"Does that feel good, darlin'?" he asked, turning his attention to her other breast.

"Mmm."

His callused palm sent wave after wave of sheer delight to every cell of her being as he moved his hand along her ribs, then down to the waistband of her silk panties. Raising his head to gaze down at her, he traced his finger along the edge of the elastic, silently asking for permission to remove the scrap of silk. Without a second thought, Natalie raised her hips for him to slowly slide them down her legs.

Pressing kisses across her collarbone, he asked, "Have you had your postnatal checkup?"

"I...uh, yes," she finally murmured. It was becoming extremely difficult to concentrate with every nerve in her body tingling from his sensual assault.

"It didn't bother you having to see a doctor for the examination?" he asked, sounding surprised.

"The gynecologist was a woman."

"So you're only bothered by male doctors?" he

asked, kissing her shoulder, her neck and the sensitive hollow behind her ear.

"Y-yes."

"Did she put you on any kind of protection?" he asked, his voice low and seductive at he moved his hand along her inner thigh.

Natalie's heart skipped several beats when he caressed her intimately. How was she supposed to think with him touching her like that?

"N-no. I hadn't planned…on needing birth control," she said breathlessly.

"Don't worry, darlin'. I'll take care of it." Giving her a kiss that made her feel as if her insides had melted, he whispered, "Be right back."

Natalie closed her eyes and tried not to think as Travis rose from the bed and crossed the hall to the master bedroom. She didn't want to consider the problems that might arise from making love with him. They still hadn't discussed how they were going to handle shared custody of Autumn, nor had they solved the mystery of who was chasing her and why.

But before she could fully analyze how difficult things could become, he returned, slipping something beneath the pillow. Then, giving her a look that left her with no doubt about how much he wanted her, he slid his underwear down his thighs and kicked them aside.

Her pulse took off at lightning speed and the blood in her veins felt as if it had turned to liquid heat. Travis's body was every bit as gorgeous as she remembered. The muscles in his wide shoulders, chest and flat stomach were well-defined. But as her gaze drifted lower, her eyes widened and her breath lodged in her lungs. She'd always found his nude body fascinating, but now she decided her memory really hadn't done justice to certain parts of him. He was impressively male, his erection proud, the softness below heavy and full. And he was looking at her as if she was the most desirable woman in the whole world.

Without a word, he climbed into bed beside her, then took her in his arms to face him. The feel of his hard maleness, the look of hungry desire in his slumberous eyes and his deep groan of pleasure as he pressed himself against her dissipated all her worry about what the future held for them.

"You feel so damn good, darlin'."

His low, sexy drawl sent a wave of goose bumps over her skin and made the coil inside her tighten with the painful ache of unfulfilled desire. She loved Travis—had never stopped loving him. And letting him know in the ultimate way a woman could express feelings for a man came as naturally to Natalie as taking her next breath.

His lips captured hers in a searing kiss as he slid his hand along her side, then down to the juncture of her thighs. His hard arousal nestled against her abdomen, the delicious friction of his chest hair teasing her sensitive nipples, the mastery of his loving touch as he parted her to stroke the tiny nub of intense sensation—all of it sent waves of heat flowing throughout her being.

Needing to touch him as he touched her, Natalie moved her hand to find him. His groan of sheer pleasure filled her with a feminine power unlike anything she'd ever known as she gently stroked his strong body.

He captured her hand with his. "Don't get me wrong. I love the way your hands feel on my body," he said, sounding as if he'd been running a marathon. "But if you don't stop, my staying power is going to be nothing more than a fond memory."

"Then make love to me, Travis," she said, still wondering if that throaty female voice was hers.

His slow grin caused a pulsing wave of longing to tighten the coil of need deep in her belly, and sent shivers of anticipation streaking up her spine. "I thought you'd never ask, darlin'."

When he reached beneath the pillow, she smiled and took the foil packet from him. "Do you mind if I help you with this?"

"I think I'd like that," he said, giving her a look that came extremely close to sending her into total meltdown.

Her fingers trembled slightly as she tore open the packaging, then carefully rolled the condom into place. She'd never taken charge before, but Travis didn't seem to mind. As soon as their protection was taken care of, he pulled her into his arms and gave her a kiss that left her feeling as if the world had gone into a fast-forward spin.

"I need to be inside of you," he said against her lips. "Is that what you want, Natalie?"

She didn't have to think twice. "Yes."

She'd no sooner gotten the word out than he parted her legs with one muscular thigh and moved over her. Brushing her hair away from her face, he gazed at her, so tenderly it brought tears to her eyes.

"Help me make us one, darlin'."

The intense need deep in her feminine core tightened at his provocative request, and reaching down, she guided him to her. As he slowly eased his lower body forward, she felt his muscles tremble and noticed the strain on his handsome face.

Natalie knew he was holding himself back, afraid that her body might still be tender from having the baby. She loved him all the more for his consideration, but she wanted to feel all of him inside of her.

"Travis, I—"

He must have known what she wanted, because he gathered her in his arms and, capturing her lips with his, buried himself within her in one smooth stroke. The feel of his hard male body on top of hers, the pleasure of once again being wrapped in the arms of the man she loved with all of her heart, and the feeling of completion from having his body joined with hers was almost overwhelming.

"Are you okay?" he asked.

She nodded. "Please, make love to me, Travis."

The flame of passion blazing bright in his hazel eyes seared her all the way to her soul, and as he set a slow pace, she knew she'd never felt more cherished than she did at that very moment. He continued to stare down at her, increasing his movements, his body heightening the delicious tension building in hers.

All too soon, Natalie felt herself tighten around him, felt her inner muscles try to hold him captive as she moved with him in the hypnotic dance of love. Apparently detecting her readiness for the fulfillment they both sought, Travis deepened his thrusts, and the coil within her suddenly snapped.

Hurtled into a storm of passion, she clung to him to keep from being swept away by the resplendent sensations coursing through her. Heat and light flashed behind her tightly closed eyes, and when he groaned her name, then plunged into her a final time, Natalie felt them become one heart, one body, one soul.

His heart pounding like a jackhammer, Trav slumped on top of Natalie, resting his forehead on her slender shoulder. "Are you…all right?" he asked, trying to catch his breath.

"I'm wonderful." Her arms tightened around him and she pressed her lips to his cheek. "That was incredible."

He shook his head. "You're incredible." Levering himself up on his elbows, he gazed down at her. "You've always been incredible, darlin'."

"Travis…"

From her expression he could tell she was unsure where things were headed between them. Truth be told, he was asking himself that same question. But at the moment, he was short on answers and wasn't about to speculate on what the future held for them.

He continued to gaze at her, his chest filled with an emotion he wasn't quite ready to put a name to. All he knew for certain was that he wanted her with him now and in the future.

Kissing her, he rolled to her side, then gathered her to him. "We'll work it out, darlin'. I promise."

The trust he saw filling her luminous eyes humbled him in ways he could never have imagined, and he made a vow then and there that he'd never do anything to give her reason to doubt him again. But before they could move forward, they needed to settle the past, and that meant ending the nightmare that had started two and a half months ago.

"Darlin', I've got to go into town later today," he said, deciding the rest of the TCC members needed to know what had taken place at the bus station in Amarillo. "You won't mind staying here with Mose and Fluffy, will you?"

"Not at all," she said, smiling. "I'm getting used to Fluffy. And Mose is a sweetheart."

Trav laughed so hard he almost choked. "I've heard Mose called a lot of things, but 'sweetheart' is a first."

She grinned. "Maybe we shouldn't tell him I called him that."

Nodding, Trav returned her grin. "It would probably be a good idea to keep it to ourselves." He gave her a quick kiss, then sat up on the side of the bed and reached for his boxer shorts. "I have a few calls to make before I leave, then I need to stop by my office at the courthouse to see if my assistant is having any kind of problems handling the caseload." Rising to his feet, he turned to face her. "While I'm gone, I have something I want you to do."

"What?"

He regretfully watched her pull up the sheet and tuck it under her arms, blocking her luscious breasts from his appreciative gaze. "I want you to pick out a movie for tonight."

She smiled as she got out of bed, wrapped the sheet around her, then walked over to him. "You want to watch another movie?"

"Yep."

"Any preferences?" she asked, placing her palm on his chest.

"N-no." Trav's blood pressure shot up a couple of dozen points from the feel of her soft hand on his sensitive skin. "Just make sure it's short." Taking her into his arms, he kissed her until they both gasped for breath. "I think it would be a good idea if we turn in early tonight."

"Catching up on sleep would probably be a good plan," she agreed, nodding.

"Darlin', going to bed and going to sleep are two different things." He pressed a quick kiss to the tip of her nose, then, while he still had the willpower, set her away from him. "And I have every intention of showing you the difference tonight."

Eight

As twilight approached, Natalie, followed closely by Fluffy, wandered out of the kitchen and over to the dry fountain in the center of the inner courtyard. She loved the way Travis's house surrounded the terra-cotta-tiled patio, which remained open to the sky above.

He'd made modifications to the traditional hacienda styling, one of them being the installation of a large doggie flap to the big wooden door on the far side of the courtyard, allowing Fluffy access to the property. She smiled when the huge dog suddenly perked up his ears and trotted over to push through the flap. He probably wanted to check out how Billy and Juan were doing down at the barn while they kept watch over one of the pregnant mares.

Walking over to sit in one of the black, wrought-iron patio chairs, she set the baby monitor on the table in front of her, then stared at the large clay pots surrounding the fountain. Even though the southwest Texas winter was mild, they were empty now. But in spring, the fountain would be flowing and the pots would be filled with bright flowers. In her mind's eye she could see graceful swallowtail butterflies gliding from one blossom to another.

Natalie caught her lower lip between her teeth to keep it from trembling. Would she still be here at the Flying W to see it?

This morning, Travis had promised her they were going to work things out. But had he been talking about a short-term relationship? Or had he been referring to a commitment between them that would last a lifetime?

When she'd called a halt to their love affair in Chicago, he'd seemed all too accepting of her decision. Once he'd handed her the Texas Cattleman's Club card, he'd walked out her door and she hadn't seen or heard from him until the recent New Year's Eve party at David and Marissa Sorrenson's.

But since he'd brought her and the baby to his ranch, Travis had acted as if they were the most important people in his life. He'd taken an extended leave from his job just to be with them, and with the exception of an occasional trip into the town of Royal, he spent every waking minute with her and Autumn.

He'd also done everything in his power to help her regain her memory.

She could tell he loved Autumn dearly, and that he was going to be a wonderful father. But could he love her as well? What would happen once the danger was over? Would he want her to stay at the Flying W and be a part of his life?

Natalie sighed. She knew he cared for her and desired her, but she wanted more. She wanted his love, and she had no intentions of settling for anything less.

The sudden, unfamiliar sound of a large dog barking interrupted her disturbing introspection and had her jumping to her feet. She'd been around Fluffy for the better part of three weeks, and it was the first time she'd ever heard him bark.

"Was that Fluff I heard?" Mose asked, hurrying out of the kitchen as fast as his arthritis would allow.

"I think so." Natalie's apprehension mounted when it was clear that he found Fluffy's behavior disturbing.

"He don't bark like that unless somethin' or somebody comes nosin' around where they ain't invited," Mose said, confirming her fears.

"Maybe it's a coyote," she said, hoping that was the case.

Mose shook his head when Fluffy continued barking. "They're around all the time and he don't pay 'em no never mind." He jerked his thumb toward the house. "You best get inside, while I get my Winchester."

Natalie's heart leaped into her throat. "D-do you really think that's necessary?"

"I don't know, gal," he admitted, following her into the kitchen. "But with Trav gone, and the trouble you've already had, I ain't takin' no chances." He turned and secured the door behind them, then switched off the lights. "You go on upstairs and lock yourself in the bedroom with the youngun'. Make sure the lights are off, so whoever is out there cain't see you movin' from room to room."

Before he finished getting the words out, Mose was crossing the kitchen to get his rifle and Natalie was running for the stairs as fast as her trembling legs would carry her.

Fear gripped her as she ran along the upstairs hall and into the bedroom she shared with Autumn. What if the people who'd chased her to Texas had found them? What if Fluffy wasn't able to scare them away?

Locking the door behind her, she hurried across the room to the crib. The phone on the bedside table rang once, but she ignored it. She had to keep them from taking her baby.

Careful not to wake Autumn, Natalie lifted her with shaky hands, then, cradling her daughter to her, entered the bathroom and secured that door as well.

Trav knew the moment he parked the SUV and killed the engine that something was amiss. The house was completely dark and he could hear Fluffy barking his head off somewhere in the distance. He couldn't tell where the dog was, but knew there had to be something terribly wrong. It was dark enough outside that there should be lights on in the house, and Fluffy only barked when he felt his territory was being threatened.

Reaching for the nine millimeter Glock he kept in the glove box, Trav released the safety, then quickly punched the speed dial on his cell phone to call the house. When Mose picked up on the first ring, Trav breathed a sigh of relief. "What the hell's going on? Why are the lights off? And what's wrong with Fluffy?"

"I don't know, boy," Mose said, sounding out of breath. "He just started tearin' up jack a minute or two ago. I'm pretty sure he's down by the barn. Soon as I got my rifle, I was fixin' to call you and tell you to get your butt home pronto."

The blood in Trav's veins turned to ice. "Where's Natalie and the baby?"

"I told her to get upstairs, lock herself and the youngun' in the bedroom, then turn the lights out so whoever's out there couldn't see inside." Mose paused to catch his breath. "I figured that was the safest place for 'em."

The relief flowing through Trav was staggering in its intensity. "Good idea," he said, thankful for the old man's wisdom. Noticing that Fluffy had stopped barking, he asked, "Do you have the house locked and the security system turned on?"

"I may be old as dirt, but I ain't stupid," Mose

grumbled, clearly insulted by Trav's question. "'Course I do.''

"Good. Stay put and guard the house, while I go check the barn.'' As an afterthought, he added, "Call Ry and tell him to get his sorry butt over here, in case I need backup.''

"Will do. And Trav?''

"What?''

"Be careful, boy.''

"I intend to, Mose,'' he said, ending the call.

He tucked the cell phone in his jacket pocket, switched off the dome light, then got out of the SUV. Thankful for his Marine Corps training and the cloud cover blocking any light from the moon, Trav veered away from the house. His dark leather jacket and black jeans against the white stucco walls would make him a sitting duck for anyone with a gun and a halfway decent aim.

Following the line of trees along the drive, he thought he heard the distinct whine of a car engine being started somewhere up on the main road, but he didn't have time to dwell on it. He didn't like the fact that the lights were out in the barn. Billy and Juan were on maternity watch with the pregnant mares, and if something had happened to the two young men, Trav would never forgive himself.

When he made it to the corner of the structure, Fluffy poked his head out of the open doorway, then whined and turned back inside. Something was definitely wrong. Ordinarily, Fluffy would have ambled out to greet him with a swipe of his huge tongue on the back of his hand.

As Trav slipped through the doors, he paused to throw the switch on the breaker box, instantly bathing the interior of the barn in light. He was fairly certain that whoever had been prowling around had moved on. Otherwise, Fluffy would still be barking loudly enough to wake the dead.

"Juan? Billy?"

Fluffy's whine coming from the far end of the barn drew his attention and Trav headed over to see what was upsetting the dog. The sight of Billy and Juan bound and gagged had him dropping to his knees to work at the knotted ropes holding them captive.

"Who did this?" he asked, removing the duct tape from their mouths.

Billy was the first to spit out the bandanna stuffed between his teeth. "I don't know who it was, boss," he said, his eyes wide. His face was abnormally pale. Even his freckles seemed to have faded. "When the overhead lights went out and I went to turn 'em back on, somebody grabbed me from behind."

"*Sí*, boss." Juan rubbed where the fibers of the rope had chafed his wrists. "The first thing I knew, I was knocked to the ground and some hombre was tying my hands behind my back. But it was too dark in here to see who it was or what he looked like."

"If Fluff hadn't come barrelin' in here like the cavalry, no tellin' what would have happened," Billy said excitedly. Some of the color was returning to his cheeks, but Trav could tell he was still keyed up, and probably would be for the rest of the evening.

"Do either of you need to see a doctor?" Trav asked, rising to his feet. When both boys shook their heads, he breathed a sigh of relief. "If you want to go on home for the night, I'll understand."

Juan and Billy exchanged a look, then Juan shook his dark head. "We said we would watch over the mares, and we will."

"Thanks, boys. I really appreciate it." Trav pointed to the barn doors. "After I leave, I want you to lock up here until daylight."

"Got it, boss," Billy said, picking up his battered Resistol and slapping it against the side of his leg to knock off the dust.

Travis took his cell phone out and punched the Re-dial button. "Whoever it was moved on," he said as soon as Mose answered. "They tied up Billy and Juan, but they're fine. Call the Royal police and tell them to send someone out here to take the boys' statements."

Just as he ended the call, Ry came jogging through the big double doors. "Hey, Trav? You all right? What the hell's going on?"

Turning, Trav met his friend in the center of the barn. "I'll explain while we're out seeing if whoever tied up Billy and Juan left any clues."

When Travis, Ryan and Fluffy finally entered the kitchen an hour after Mose let her know the danger was over, Natalie felt a little less shaky. But not much. Even though she had the baby monitor in hand and knew the baby was safely tucked in her crib upstairs, she had a compelling need to visibly check on Autumn every five minutes to make sure no one had taken her.

Apparently, the remnants of her fear must have been more evident than she'd realized, because Travis immediately walked over to her and folded her in his arms. "Everything's fine now, darlin'. Whoever was out there took off as soon as Fluffy showed up."

"Are Billy and Juan all right?" she asked, burrowing deeper into his protective embrace.

"They were a little shook up, but they're none the worse for wear," he said, tightening his arms around her. "Wayne Vincente, the Royal police chief, took their statements, but that's about all he could do. Whoever tied them up was smart. He didn't leave any kind of evidence behind for Wayne to go on."

"Well, it looks like everything's under control here," Ryan said, drawing Natalie's attention. For the first time since he'd entered the kitchen with Travis, she noticed he held a rifle. "I think I'll head toward the diner. I have a sudden craving for some of Manny's stick-to-your-ribs chili."

Turning, she watched the two men exchange a meaningful look before Travis gave an almost imperceptible nod. "Tell the rest of the guys I'll try to make it to next month's chili-fest."

Ryan nodded. Then, smiling, he tipped his hat to

her. "Take care, Natalie." To Travis, he added, "I'll see you at the regular TCC meeting day after tomorrow."

"He's going to tell the others what happened here tonight, isn't he?" she asked once Ryan closed the door behind him.

"I think I'll mosey on to my room," Mose said, looking overly tired. "I'm gettin' too danged old for this kind of shenanigans."

Natalie watched the old man limp to his room and close the door before she turned her attention back to Travis. "What do you and Ryan think the others could do about what happened here tonight that the police can't?"

"It's our monthly chili night," Travis answered evasively. "Ry rarely misses it."

Natalie shook her head. "Don't patronize me. I know you and the other members of the TCC have been investigating what happened to me the night I arrived in Royal. From what Marissa, Tara and Carrie have told me, the TCC regularly assists the authorities in solving crimes, or preventing them from happening."

He continued to stare at her for several tense moments, his expression wary. "I'm sure he'll fill them in, and they'll discuss it, but—"

"Never mind," she said, shaking her head. She could tell he didn't want to talk about it, and she wasn't sure she wanted to know what the men were up to, anyway. "All I care about is that no one gets hurt because of me."

Travis reached for her again. "Darlin', I don't want you worrying about anything but taking care of Autumn and regaining your memory." His smile sent a shiver up her spine. "And I'll be right here to take care of both of you." Brushing his lips over hers, he whispered, "Now, let's go upstairs so I can hold you and show you just how much I missed you today."

Her knees felt as if the tendons had turned to putty. "That sounds very…interesting."

"Oh, I promise it will be," he said, grinning as he guided her toward the stairs. When they entered her bedroom, he took her into his arms. "I'm going to make you forget what happened tonight. I want you to think only of how I'm making you feel."

The look in his hazel eyes and the sensation of his hard body pressed to hers sent tremors of need straight to her core. "I doubt that I'll be able to think of anything else."

He started to lower his mouth to hers, but the sound of their daughter awakening had them both taking deep breaths.

"I think Autumn wants her evening bottle," Natalie sighed.

Travis rested his forehead against hers. "Why don't you take a nice relaxing bath while I feed her and get her settled in for the night?"

A long, soaking bath sounded like heaven. "But

you got up with her this morning. It wouldn't be fair for—''

He placed his index finger to her lips. ''I don't mind. If you'll remember, I told you that I would be here to take care of both of you.'' He gave her a quick kiss, then stepped back. ''And that's just what I intend to do, darlin'.''

As Natalie watched him pick up their daughter, she smiled. ''I have a feeling Autumn is going to have her daddy wrapped around her little finger.''

He shook his head as he walked back to stand in front of her. Giving her a kiss that made her weak in the knees, then kissing the baby's soft chubby cheek, he grinned. ''Darlin', Autumn can't wrap me around her little finger. I'm already there.''

When Trav placed his sleeping daughter in the crib, he stood looking down at the most precious sight he'd ever seen—his little girl. His chest filled with such emotion he thought it just might burst. He couldn't believe how much more meaning his life had taken on in the past few weeks.

Glancing over at the bed, he smiled at the sight of his child's mother. Natalie lay on top of the comforter, sound asleep. After taking her bath, she must have put on her robe and lain down while waiting on him to come back upstairs with the baby.

He walked over to stand beside the bed. God, she was beautiful. Her hair was spread over the pillow like strands of golden-brown silk, and her long dark lashes looked like tiny feathery fans against her perfect porcelain cheeks.

How had he managed to stay away from her for the past eleven months?

After he'd returned from his mission in Chicago, he'd found himself spending most of his days and all of his nights thinking about her. He'd lain awake for hours wondering what she was doing, who she was with and if she ever thought about him.

But he'd been too stubborn to pick up the phone and call her. He'd convinced himself that their month-long involvement had been fun, but that sooner or later it had been destined to end. But had it?

Truth to tell, his pride had taken a direct hit when she'd sent him packing. It had been the first time in his adult life that a woman had called a halt to a relationship with him, instead of the other way around. Until he met Natalie, he'd always been the one to decide that things were getting too serious.

But looking back on it, he realized she'd always been different. He'd been entranced from the minute he'd first laid eyes on her, whereas she'd resisted his initial efforts to get acquainted with him. He shook his head at how foolish he must have looked to her. It had taken him the rest of the evening, drinking about a gallon of the worst greasy-spoon coffee he'd ever had the misfortune to taste, before he'd managed to charm her into letting him walk her home that night.

As he continued to stare down at her, she smiled

and murmured his name in her sleep. Now that she was back in his life, how would he ever survive if she returned to Chicago after the danger to her and the baby was over?

His heart stalled and his next breath lodged in his lungs as the realization slammed into him like a charging bull. He loved her—had probably loved her from the moment he'd met her. He'd just been too blind to see it.

But instead of the panic he would have expected to accompany the emotion rapidly invading every fiber of his being, a deep peace like nothing he'd ever known swept over him. He'd never had anything feel more right than the knowledge that he loved Natalie.

Now all he needed to do was think of the best way to go about telling her how he felt. The timing needed to be perfect and the setting just right. Something as important as declaring his feelings and asking the woman he loved to marry him would have to have some serious thought put into it.

Trav smiled as he pulled a foil packet out of his hip pocket and laid it within easy reach on the nightstand. He continued to gaze at Natalie as he unfastened the snaps on his chambray shirt, pulled it from the waistband of his jeans, then reached for his fly. Until he could come up with the perfect plan to tell her how he felt, he had every intention of showing her.

Nine

Natalie's eyes fluttered open when a pair of strong arms gathered her to a wide bare chest. The clean masculine scent, the taste of the firm male lips on hers and the sound of a deep baritone whispering her name made her shiver with longing. Travis.

Snuggling close, she smiled. "Did you get Autumn settled for the night?"

"Yep." He ran his lips from her cheek down to the hollow behind her ear. "And now that I've taken care of her, I'm going to take care of her mother."

Goose bumps pebbled her skin as his warm breath tickled the sensitive skin along her neck. "Wh-what did you have in mind?"

When he leaned back to look at her, the heat in his

gaze stole her breath. "I'm going to love you until we both forget where one of us ends and the other begins." He gave her a teasing kiss. "Then I'm going to hold you while you sleep, wake up with you in my arms tomorrow morning and love you all over again."

"I like the way that sounds," she said, tracing the definition of muscles across his wide shoulders with her fingertip.

"I'm going to make sure you like the way it feels even more," he said, his smile filled with promise.

Her entire body tingled to life at his candor, and she felt warmed to the depths of her soul when he lowered his head to capture her mouth with his. He encouraged her to open for him, and when she parted her lips for his entry, he slipped his tongue inside to stroke her with such care it left her breathless.

As he allowed her to taste his passion, the depth of his need, her own desire blossomed like a flower opening up to a warm spring sun. When he reverently caressed her, she knew that no other man would ever touch every place in her heart the way he did.

He ran his finger along the lapel of her robe, parting it when he reached the valley between her breasts. At some point he must have untied the sash, because the garment fell open, exposing her nude body to his loving touch. But Natalie didn't mind. She wanted to feel him touching her, wanted to have him hold her as if she was the most fragile of objects.

"Your skin is so soft, so smooth." He lightly

traced his finger down the slope of her breast. "It feels like fine satin."

His gaze held hers, and when he touched the hardened tip, it felt as if a tiny charge of electricity shot through her. Her nipple tightened further and she caught her lip between her teeth to keep from moaning.

"Let me hear you, Natalie," he rasped. "I want to know when I'm making you feel good, darlin'."

He'd no sooner gotten the words out than he lowered his head to take the taut peak into his mouth. At the first touch of his tongue to her sensitive flesh, swirls of heat coursed through her, followed closely by a delicious little flutter deep in her belly. He circled each of her nipples with his tongue, then nibbled at them with his lips, and Natalie didn't even try to hold back the sound of her pleasure.

"That's it, darlin'," he murmured against her breast. "Tell me how it feels."

If she could have gotten her vocal cords to work, she might have told him that she felt as if he'd ignited a flame inside her. But, incapable of speech, she could only manage a heartfelt sigh.

His deep baritone vibrated against her abdomen as he kissed his way from her breast to her navel. "I'm going to love every inch of you."

She shivered when he tickled the indentation with his tongue, then continued nibbling on down her body. But when she realized where he was going with his sensual exploration, she sucked in a sharp breath. "Travis—"

"It's all right, Natalie." He raised his head to look at her, and the searing light in his hazel eyes stole her breath. "I want to love you in every way a man can love a woman. Will you let me do that?"

How could she refuse when he was looking at her with such passion, such desire?

"Y-yes."

His smile caused her temperature to rise and a tremor to streak up her spine. But when he lowered his head to give her the most intimate kiss, her body began to tremble and her heart pounded against her ribs with a sultry beat. Closing her eyes, she felt every nerve in her body leap to life when he found the tiny nub of pleasure and teased it tenderly.

Trav felt Natalie tremble against him, heard her whisper his name as he continued to caress her intimately. He could tell she was reaching the point of no return when she gripped the comforter with both hands and began to move restlessly beneath him.

Slowly kissing his way back up her stomach to her collarbone, he slid his hand along her side to cup her full breast. He loved the contrast of her smooth feminine skin against his callused hand, loved the way her nipple peaked as if begging for his touch.

She grasped his shoulders, her nails scoring his skin as he chafed the tip with the pad of his thumb. "Travis, please!"

"Not yet," he said, loving the deep rose of passion coloring her cheeks, the way she arched into his hands, seeking his touch.

She opened her eyes to gaze up at him, and the hungry desire so evident there caused his body to throb with a need that quickly had him gritting his teeth and struggling to hang on to his control. "You're gorgeous when you're turned on, darlin'."

"I...can't take...much more," she panted, her husky voice sending fire racing through his veins. "I...need you."

He kissed her elegant neck and the delicate hollow at the base of it as he pressed his lower body to her thigh. "What is it you need, darlin?"

"You. Inside of me. Please!"

Sliding his hand along her side to the roundness of her hip, then down to the crisp, dark brown curls at the apex of her thighs, he dipped his finger inside to stroke her to a frenzied passion. "I want to make this a night you'll remember."

The look she gave him was almost his undoing. "You're driving me crazy, Travis."

Smiling, he started to tell her how much he loved her, how he wanted them to be together this way every night for the rest of their lives, but he held back. If he declared his love now, she might think it was nothing more than words spoken in the heat of the moment. And when he told her how he felt, he wanted there to be no doubt in her mind about his sincerity.

But all thought faded when she reached down to

take him in her soft hands. As she caressed, stroked and teased him, Trav had to struggle to maintain the last scrap of his sanity.

"Darlin', don't get me wrong," he said, gasping for breath. "I love the way your hands feel, but right now, that's not a good idea."

"Then love me."

Trav reached for the foil packet he'd placed on the nightstand. He quickly arranged their protection, then pulled her back into his arms and settled himself between her slender legs.

Unable to find the right words to express what she meant to him, he let his body show her how much he cherished and adored her. Slowly pushing forward, Trav closed his eyes and gritted his teeth as he held himself in check. His body was urging him to bury himself inside of her. But this was only the second time Natalie had made love since having Autumn, and he didn't want to rush things in case her body was still tender.

But apparently she had other ideas. Suddenly, and with no warning, she wrapped her arms around his shoulders at the same time she locked her long, slender legs around his hips, encouraging him to fill her completely.

Caught off guard, Trav groaned and, giving in to her demand, sank himself to the hilt in her soft heat. The blood rushing through his veins caused his ears to roar, and he had to fight the red haze of passion threatening to swamp him.

Holding completely still, he gritted his teeth and willed himself to slow down. He wanted to draw out their lovemaking, wanted to bring Natalie immeasurable pleasure. But she was making it damn hard to hold himself in check.

When he finally felt that he had a modicum of control, he smiled down at her. "Look at me, darlin'."

As her gaze met his, he pulled back, then eased forward, setting a slow pace. Gradually quickening his thrusts, he found his chest filling with emotion as Natalie met and matched him stroke for stroke in the age-old dance. But all too soon he felt her body tighten around his, straining to hold him captive as she reached for the pinnacle of her release.

"Just let it happen, darlin'," he murmured.

A split second later, her inner muscles quivered around him, and he watched as the storm of her passion overtook her. Softly moaning his name, she clung to him with a fierceness that thrilled him, and he felt himself being swept into the vortex with her.

Trav groaned her name, his body stiffening to an almost painful degree before he ground himself against her one last time and gave up his essence in a mind-shattering explosion of pleasure.

Several moments later, when he finally had the strength to lever himself away from her, he smiled down at the woman he loved with every fiber of his being. "Are you all right?"

The look in her eyes robbed him of breath. "I'm wonderful."

"Yes, you are," he said, moving to her side.

"I wasn't talking about me being wonderful," she said, her smile warming him all the way to his soul. "I meant I felt—"

Gathering her to him, he chuckled. "I know what you meant." He gave her a kiss that left them both gasping for breath. "But I happen to think you're the most beautiful, most amazing woman I've ever known, and I have every intention of spending the rest of the night showing you just how special you are."

"I think you mean that," she said breathlessly.

He pressed his rapidly recovering body against her and watched a renewed hunger light her pretty violet eyes. "I never say anything I don't mean, darlin'. But it will be my pleasure, and yours, to convince you of just how sincere I really am."

"I might take a lot of convincing," she said, her grin impish.

"I'm counting on it," he retorted, lowering his mouth to hers.

And for the rest of the night, Trav delighted both of them in pleading his case.

"Boss, I think you'd better come and take a look at this," Billy said, sliding to a halt just inside the barn doors.

Trav looked up from checking on Sugar Babe. The sorrel mare was in labor and had been for several hours, but as yet showed no signs of any real progress. If something didn't happen in the next hour, he was going to be making a call to the vet.

"It won't be much longer, girl," he said, patting the horse's neck. Letting himself out of the stall, Trav refastened the webbed gate. "What did you find?"

Billy shook his head. "Wasn't me. Juan found it. We both think it has something to do with what happened the other night."

The back of Trav's neck tingled as he followed the boy outside and around the end of the barn. It had been three days since some thug tied up the boys, and Trav and Ry had been over every inch of the area with a fine-tooth comb—the night the incident occurred, as well as the next day. If there was anything out here now, someone had to have returned during the past two nights.

"What do you make of this, boss?" Juan asked, when Trav and Billy joined him about twenty yards past the barn.

The dead winter grass had been trampled and the stub of a fat cigar lay discarded a few feet away. Knowing that Juan's and Billy's mothers would skin them alive if either of the boys took up smoking, Trav didn't even bother asking if the cigar belonged to one of them.

"Did either of you touch anything?" he asked, pulling his cell phone from the case attached to his belt.

Juan shook his head. "No, we figured you and Mr. Evans would want to check it out first."

''Good thinking.'' Trav punched in the Royal Police Department's number. While he waited for it to ring, he jerked his thumb toward the barn. ''Billy, you stay with Sugar Babe while Juan calls the vet. She needs help foaling.''

Both boys turned and walked back to the barn entrance as Trav's call was put through to the police chief. Explaining what had been discovered, Trav was assured an investigator would be right out to collect the evidence. They were hoping to recover some DNA samples from the cigar stub, but Trav knew that at this point it would only rule out who the culprit wasn't, not who he was. Unless, of course, the guy had his DNA profiled by one of the major law enforcement agencies and it showed up during a computer analysis.

Trav muttered a vehement curse. Neither option was appealing. On one hand, if the guy didn't have his DNA on file, they'd be no closer to discovering his identity. And if he did, it meant he had a record and was most likely an extremely dangerous career criminal.

''Boss, we've got more trouble,'' Billy called out.

What the hell else could go wrong? Trav wondered as he turned to walk toward the young man.

''It looks like the barn's phone lines have been cut,'' the boy said before Trav could ask what the problem was.

Seething with anger, Trav followed Billy over to the side of the barn where the phone cable came up out of the ground. Sure enough, about half the distance from the ground to the junction box, the conduit had been sawed in two and the wires severed.

"When was the last time you or Juan used this phone?" Trav asked.

"Last night around eight or nine," Billy answered. His face turned almost as red as his hair. "I know I probably shouldn't have done it from here, since I was workin' and all. But Juan dared me to call Ali Hendricks for a date Saturday night."

Trav nodded. "So the line had to have been cut after that."

"Yes, sir." Billy looked as if he expected to get his butt chewed for making a personal call while working.

Deciding there was nothing he could do until the police investigator arrived, Trav again pulled his cell phone from its case. He still needed to get hold of the vet for Sugar Babe. His frustration mounted when he noticed the power symbol on the tiny screen was all but nonexistent, indicating that the battery was going dead.

"I'll have to go up to the house and call the vet."

"Uh, boss?"

"What, Billy?" Trav turned toward the house.

"I'm real sorry about calling Ali on your time."

Taking pity on the boy, Trav grinned. "What did she say?"

Billy looked wary. "Uh, she said she'd go, but only if I found a date for her best friend, Megan."

"So did you find somebody?" Trav asked.

Billy nodded, looking relieved. "Turns out Juan has the hots for Megan, and she's had a crush on him for ages."

Trav caught Billy by the arm before the boy reentered the barn. "Don't worry about making calls while you're working late. As long as you don't let it interfere with watching the mares, or getting your chores done, I don't care."

Billy's grin stretched from ear to ear. "Thanks, boss. You're the best."

Once the boy went back into the barn, Trav continued on to the house. His mind was already back on who had been skulking around his property, tying up a couple of innocent kids and cutting phone lines. Whoever it was, he'd be sorry he'd ever been born once Trav got his hands on the son of a bitch.

Entering the kitchen, Trav found his mood improving considerably at the sight of Natalie working alongside Mose as they prepared dinner. "What are we having?" he asked, deciding not to tell her about the most recent trouble.

The smile she sent his way caused his jeans to feel as if they were a couple of sizes too small. "I'm not certain what Mose is making, but he assures me it tastes as good as it smells."

Trav picked up the cordless phone from the counter. "He'd say that no matter what it is."

"Well, now. For the last five years I've been fixin'

your suppers and I never did see you turn one of 'em down,'' the man said, clearly insulted.

''That's because all the meals you make are good, Mose.'' Trav dialed the veterinarian's office. ''I've had no room to complain.''

''Good save,'' Natalie said, grinning.

Trav winked at her. ''I thought so.'' When the vet picked up on the third ring, he turned his attention to the business at hand. ''Mac, could you come out to the Flying W? I have a mare in labor and she's showing signs of complications. I'm afraid that if something's not done soon, we're going to lose the colt, and maybe even her.''

He heard a startled cry, followed closely by the sound of a bowl shattering against the tiled floor. Turning, Trav felt his heart stall at the sight of Natalie trembling uncontrollably, her complexion ghostly pale.

''I've got to go,'' he said, hanging up on the vet. ''Natalie, what's wrong?'' He started toward her, and when her knees buckled, he caught her to him. ''Darlin', talk to me.''

''They didn't die,'' she cried, clutching at his shirt. ''My God, Travis, he was stealing them to sell on the black market.''

Ten

His heart pounding so hard it felt as if it might crack a couple of ribs, Trav swung Natalie up, cradling her to his chest, and started for the stairs. He knew without asking that her memory had returned, and the events were more unnerving than either of them could have imagined.

"The phone's out down at the barn," he called over his shoulder to Mose. "Go tell the boys they'll have to help the vet with Sugar. You stay down there and wait for the detective."

The old man looked confused. "The police are comin' out here? What for?"

"Billy and Juan will explain."

Trav took Natalie to his bedroom instead of the

room she shared with Autumn. She was extremely upset, and he had a feeling it might get worse before it got better. He didn't want to run the risk of them disturbing the baby. One upset female at a time was about all he could handle, and at the moment, Natalie definitely needed him more than Autumn did.

"It's going to be all right, darlin'." Holding her close, he sank down in one of the big armchairs in the sitting area of the master suite. "You and the baby are safe. I promise I won't let anyone hurt either of you."

When her sobs quieted a bit, she shuddered against him. "My God, Travis, he was…going to sell… Autumn."

The blood in Trav's veins turned to ice. Someone had tried to steal their daughter to sell?

Struggling to remain calm, he cupped Natalie's face in his palms. The anguish he saw in the depths of her eyes was almost more than he could take.

"Darlin', I want you to take a deep breath and start at the beginning," he said, careful to keep his voice even. Right now, she needed a calming strength, not a man filled with enough rage to take apart an armored tank with his bare hands. "Tell me the doctor's name."

"Dr. Roman Birkenfeld." She shuddered violently. "When I went for a checkup shortly after I lost my job at the diner, I asked if the Birkenfeld Birthing Clinic had some type of monthly plan I could use to pay for the birth." She closed her eyes for a moment as if to collect herself for what she was about to say. "When he learned I was out of work, he offered me a position as a secretary and receptionist at the clinic." She shivered. "But it didn't take long for me to realize that something was terribly wrong."

"What did you find out, darlin'?"

Trav knew that having to relive the events that sent her running to find him was going to be one of the hardest things she'd ever had to do. But she needed to get it out in order to deal with it, and he needed as much information as possible for the TCC members to follow through and bring whoever was doing this to justice.

"The number of babies dying at birth was alarming," she said, her voice shaky. "Three were lost in one week—all due to complications during birth, and all to single mothers with no family."

"None of the married women lost their babies?" He was by no means schooled on the percentages of infants dying at birth, but even he could figure out that something wasn't right about the ratio.

She shook her head. "A married woman hadn't lost a baby at the clinic in almost a year."

"I thought they only allowed women with normal, low-risk pregnancies to deliver in birthing clinics," he said, thinking aloud. "And if a woman did start having problems she was transported to a hospital."

"That's what happened with the few married women who had trouble while I was working there." Natalie thought for a moment. "And I even remember one or two single women being transferred because of complications. But these babies supposedly died during the actual birth, from last-minute complications.''

Trav frowned. ''Supposedly?''

He watched her bite her lip to keep it from trembling as she nodded. ''The women were told their babies died, but they were actually born alive and healthy.''

''Are you sure?'' he asked, his gut twisting into a painful knot. ''What happened to the babies?''

''Dr. Birkenfeld…sold them,'' she answered, shuddering violently.

The implications of what Natalie was telling him were not only sickening, they were staggering. Women were being told they had lost their babies in order for an unscrupulous doctor to make a profit?

''How did you find all this out, darlin'?'' Trav asked gently.

Apparently unable to sit still, Natalie stood up and began to pace the room. ''After I noticed how many babies were dying, I discovered that every woman who'd lost a baby had a numbered code beside her name in the data system.'' She wrapped her arms around herself when she turned to face him. ''I did a search and found hidden files with the sex of the infant born to each mother, and the name of the couple who had…bought the baby.''

The realization that Autumn had almost been one of those babies slammed into Trav like a physical blow. If he ever came face-to-face with Birkenfeld, he'd tear the man apart limb by limb.

But as he contemplated what Natalie had told him, he frowned. "Darlin', do you know how Birkenfeld was getting away with this?"

She nodded. "Just before the baby was born, he would tell the mother that complications had developed and he was going to have to administer a sedative." Tears filled her eyes. "Then, once the woman was unconscious, he delivered the baby without her knowing if it survived. When she woke up, he would tell her that her baby had died while being born."

Trav rose to his feet and took her into his arms. "If you knew this, why didn't you notify the police? And why weren't you able to avoid the same thing happening to you?"

"I tried, but I went into labor before I could confront him," she said, clutching the front of Travis's shirt. "I was at work when my water broke. I think Birkenfeld must have known that I'd discovered something, because when I kept insisting that I wanted to go to the hospital instead of having Autumn at the clinic, he administered a sedative. After I woke up, I realized I'd already given birth."

The knot in Trav's gut tightened even more at the thought of what Natalie had gone through. "Did he try to tell you the same thing he told the other women?"

Nodding, she laid her head against his chest, and her tears wetting his shirt burned him all the way to his soul. "After the nurse let him know that I was conscious and asking to see my baby, he came in and told me there had been problems during the delivery and he hadn't been able to save my little girl."

"But I don't understand how he could get away with it, unless he had help." Trav tightened his hold on her. "Do you know if any of the nurses were aware of what he was doing?"

"He had only one nurse." Natalie paused as if trying to remember. "Her name was Mary Campbell and I'm pretty sure she was helping him." Natalie leaned back to look up at Travis. "She had to be in on it with him, because she was present for every delivery and took care of the infant while the doctor finished attending the mother."

"I think you're probably right," Trav agreed. He brushed a strand of hair from her eyes with his index finger. "Do you remember anything else, darlin'? How did you manage to get away from there with Autumn?"

"He told me the same thing I assume he told every one of those women—that since I was so obviously distraught about the loss of my baby, and because he knew I didn't have the money for a proper burial, he would take care of disposing of the body by having it cremated." Trav felt a tremor run through her, then she took a deep breath. "As he left the room, he told me he would send in the nurse to give me another sedative…. I almost lost our baby, Travis," she said brokenly.

Her body began to tremble again, and knowing her knees were about to give way, he led her back to the chair, sat down and pulled her onto his lap. Pure fury shot through him as he thought of all the anguish the bastard had caused the women.

"But you didn't lose her, Natalie." He wiped a tear from her cheek with the pad of his thumb. "She's here where she belongs, and no one is going to take her away from us."

"But you don't understand," she said, shivering uncontrollably. "I managed to slip away before the nurse could give me the shot, but I couldn't find Autumn."

Trav's heart stuttered. "Then how…"

"I knew if they found me, they'd give me the sedative and I'd lose my baby forever." A look of determination filled her eyes. "Before Mary came back into the room, I changed into my clothes, then hid in a storage closet across from Dr. Birkenfeld's office. They searched for me for several minutes, then I heard him tell Mary they didn't have time to waste. That she should get the baby and the diaper bag, while he called the couple who were going to…buy Autumn. He told her they'd be taking a flight to deliver her to her new parents and collect the rest of the money so he could pay off his loan."

"You followed them," he guessed, knowing that was exactly what she'd done.

His stomach twisted even tighter when he thought of Natalie having to go after the pair alone, and what might have happened to her. Aside from the danger to her health after just giving birth, the unscrupulous doctor and nurse could have killed her to keep her from revealing their illegal activities.

She nodded. "When I caught up to them at the airport, I waited until Mary took Autumn into the women's rest room to change her. I followed, and when she leaned over to take a diaper out of the bag, I shoved her down, grabbed the baby and the diaper bag and ran."

"Birkenfeld didn't try to stop you?" Trav asked incredulously.

"He was busy at the ticket counter," she said, shaking her head. "I managed to disappear into a crowd of people who had just claimed their bags and were headed out to find taxis."

"So you had enough money with you for the fare?"

Shaking her head, she grimaced. "I dropped my purse in the rest room. I had to ask a nice older couple if I could share their cab." She looked him square in the eye and he could tell that it had stung her pride to ask for monetary help of any kind. "I hated having to do that. But they were so nice. They even paid the driver to take me to the bus station after he dropped them off at their hotel."

"If you didn't have any money, how did you pay for the bus ticket?" Trav asked, frowning.

For the first time since her memory returned, she gave him a half smile. "I discovered a few hundred thousand dollars tucked inside the diaper bag that I hadn't realized was there.''

Trav couldn't help but grin. "So you used Birkenfeld's money to escape."

She nodded. "I don't like taking anything that's not mine, but I needed it to save my baby."

He shook his head. "The money doesn't belong to Birkenfeld, anyway. I'm sure it's what he collected from selling the newborns.''

Her lower lip trembled. "I feel so sorry for those other women who think their babies died. I just wish there was something I could do to help them get their children back.''

Trav nodded, but remained silent. He couldn't tell her for sure, but he had a good idea that the TCC would investigate and try to help the authorities recover the stolen babies for the mothers who had been victimized by Birkenfeld.

"So it was Birkenfeld and the Campbell woman who accosted you at the Amarillo bus station?" he asked, needing to find out the rest of what she remembered.

"Yes, I'm certain of it." Natalie chewed on her lower lip. "I remember seeing them in the bus station, but I didn't think they'd seen me." She sighed. "Apparently I was wrong."

"Do you remember anything else, darlin'?"

"I recall struggling with Mary to keep her from taking Autumn after I was hit from behind." When Natalie raised her gaze to meet his, the look in her eyes caused him to suck in a sharp breath. "I have no memory of how I got on the right bus. But I do remember reaching into my coat pocket for the card you gave me and thinking that I had to stay conscious. I knew I had to get to you, because I knew you wouldn't let them take our baby."

Trav's chest swelled with emotion. Natalie might not have realized it at the time, but she hadn't lost all of her faith in him when she'd kicked him out of her apartment that night almost a year ago. She'd known that if she could get to him, he'd keep her and Autumn safe. And if she would let him, he fully intended to spend the rest of his life doing just that.

But even as his heart filled to bursting with love for Natalie, his gut burned with a fury he'd never known before. Birkenfeld and his nurse had to be caught, and the sooner the better. Travis hated having to leave Natalie and the baby, but he needed to call an emergency meeting of the TCC and get them started on the investigation immediately. Once he'd done that, he could put his plans into action for this evening, and concentrate on making the moment perfect when he asked her to be his wife.

"What do Birkenfeld and this Campbell woman look like?" he asked. A detailed description would go a long way in helping apprehend the pair.

"Mary is average height with blond hair." Natalie stopped to think. "I can't remember her eye color for sure, but I think it might be blue. Dr. Birkenfeld is tall and thin, with coffee-brown hair." Natalie tilted her head. "I think he's probably in his mid to late thirties and he's reasonably handsome. But..." she shivered "...his brown eyes are empty."

"What do you mean, darlin'?"

She sighed. "It's hard to explain, but it's almost like he has no soul. You know how when you look into someone's eyes you see their personality and character?"

Trav nodded.

"Dr. Birkenfeld doesn't have that. His eyes are vacant."

"I swear he'll never get near you again," Trav vowed. He gave her a fervent kiss. "Darlin', I need to run a few errands—"

Placing her finger to his lips, she gave him a watery smile. "I know you need to let the other men know that I've recovered my memory." The lone tear trickling down her cheek caused his chest to constrict painfully. "Dr. Birkenfeld has to be stopped, Travis. He can't be allowed to continue what he's doing to innocent women and their babies."

Trav tenderly wiped the droplet away. "Darlin', I promise you that Birkenfeld's days are numbered."

"He's doing what?" Ry asked incredulously.

"Birkenfeld is telling women their babies died at birth, then he's selling the infants to couples who either don't qualify for legal adoption or don't want to go through the normal channels because of the waiting period," Trav answered.

Seated in the private meeting room of the TCC clubhouse, Trav watched the expressions on his fellow members' faces as he recounted what Natalie had recalled. Their reactions ranged from shock to outrage. But none was stronger than the sheik's. Although his demeanor remained as stoic as ever, the fury burning in Darin's obsidian eyes was formidable. Trav had no idea why, but it seemed as if the man took the news of babies being stolen personally.

"We've got to take this bastard down," David Sorrenson said, sitting forward in his chair.

Clint Andover gave a low whistle. "I knew whatever happened to Natalie had to be bad, but this is worse than I imagined."

Alex Kent nodded. "We not only have to stop Birkenfeld, we need to help these other women locate their babies."

"What we need to do first is find Birkenfeld," Ry interjected. "And whoever he has helping him here in Royal."

"Yeah, it's clear that he's hired someone to do his dirty work," David agreed. "Natalie's description of Birkenfeld doesn't match the one Marissa gave me of the thug who tried to kidnap the baby at the hospital two months ago."

"Alex, you still have contacts in the FBI," Trav said, thinking aloud. "Why don't you get in touch with them and see if this doctor has a record, or if anyone knows anything about the Birkenfeld Birthing Clinic."

"If you have a lead on this man, I will find him,"
Darin announced. The determination Trav detected in
the sheik's tone left no doubt that Darin would travel
to the ends of the earth if he had to in order to bring
Birkenfeld to justice. And that it wouldn't be pretty
when the sheik found him.

"While Alex contacts his friends at the Bureau, I
think Clint and I need to do some checking around
here," David said. "With someone prowling around
the Flying W, it's obvious that Natalie and the baby
are still in danger."

"I'm betting it's the same SOB who torched Tara's
place," Clint said, his voice hard. "If I get the
chance—"

"You can have him after I get finished with him,"
Trav interrupted, his tone just as unyielding. "But
don't count on there being a whole lot left."

"What can I do to help?" Ry asked earnestly.

Trav had to bite the inside of his cheek to keep
from smiling. Ry had just given him the opening he'd
been looking for. "Keep your cell phone with you in
case I need to get hold of you like I did the other
night." He paused. "And if you could continue to
keep an eye on Carrie, I'd appreciate it."

"You're starting to sound like a damn recording,
Trav." Ry groaned. "You know I'll watch out for
Carrie-bear, but she's going to despise the sight of me
before this is over."

Alex laughed. "Where's all that confidence you've
been telling us you have, Evans?"

"Carrie's different," Ry said defensively.

Trav watched his best friend's face turn red all the way to the roots of his hair. He'd been right. Ry was beginning to notice Carrie had grown into a woman and was no longer the freckle-faced little girl who used to follow them everywhere they went.

"So you'll help me out?" Trav prompted.

Ry looked insulted. "You know better than to ask a damn fool question like that. Of course I'll keep an eye on Carrie."

Before the others could start ribbing Ry about being a baby-sitter or a watchdog, Trav stood up. He didn't like leaving Natalie and the baby alone any longer than he had to. Besides, he needed to get back and put his plans in motion. By the time they went to bed tonight, he wanted it cut and dried that he and Natalie were going to be joining the Sorrensons and Andovers in the sacred state of holy matrimony.

"I need to get back to the ranch and make sure nothing else happens." At the door he turned back. "If any of you find out anything—"

"You'll be the first to know," the other men said in unison.

Trav nodded. "And don't worry about Carrie's whereabouts tonight, Ry. I'm taking her home with me to baby-sit Autumn."

"You're taking Natalie out somewhere?" Ry asked, frowning. "Isn't that a little dangerous, since you don't know where Birkenfeld is, or who's been prowling around the Flying W?"

"I didn't say I was taking Natalie anywhere." Unable to stop a wide grin, Trav added just before he closed the door behind him, "But she and I will be occupied for most of the evening."

Instead of feeling drained from the emotional ordeal of reliving what had taken place almost three months ago, Natalie felt as if she'd been set free. As horrible as the memories were, she no longer had to wonder what had been so bad that it sent her running to Royal, Texas, looking for Travis. Deep down, she'd always known that he could be trusted to keep her and the baby safe, and that she still loved him with all her heart.

As she sat in the rocking chair, gazing down at the baby in her arms, Autumn gave her a little half smile. She looked so much like Travis. From her tiny dimples to the cowlick in her light brown hair, there was no denying that she was his child. And Natalie knew beyond a shadow of a doubt that he loved the baby dearly. But how did he feel about her?

Natalie knew he cared for her. But that didn't mean he loved her. Once the danger was over, where would they be? Would he want her to go back to Chicago?

As she contemplated what would happen after Dr. Birkenfeld was apprehended, and what the future might hold for her and Travis, Natalie heard a set of footsteps on the stairs, then someone coming down the hall. When she looked up, Carrie stood at her bedroom door.

"Hi, Carrie," Natalie said, somewhat confused. "I thought you had plans for the evening with your friend Stephanie."

"We were just going to the Royal Diner for coffee and some girl talk." Carrie shrugged as she walked over to the rocking chair. "Nothing that couldn't be put off for another night." Smiling, she leaned down to hug Natalie. "Trav said you remembered what happened."

"Did he tell you—"

"Everything." Carrie nodded. "I'm so glad you managed to get away before that horrible man…" Her voice caught, and shaking her head, she reached for Autumn. "I can't even bear…to say it."

When Carrie lifted Autumn to her shoulder, Natalie rose from the chair. "I know. I can't believe how close I came to…losing her."

"Don't think about it, Natalie," Carrie said, hugging the baby close. "It's all in the past now."

Nodding, Natalie moved to fold some of the baby's clothes she'd laundered earlier. "I'm trying to focus on the future."

"Good idea." Travis's sister grinned. "You know what I think would be an even better idea?"

Her delighted expression was so infectious, Natalie couldn't help but smile. "What's that?"

"I think you should go downstairs and relax, while I spend some quality time with my niece." Carrie's hazel eyes danced with excitement, making Natalie wonder what the woman was up to.

"But—"

"I'm not taking no for an answer," she insisted. "Travis is back from town. Why don't the two of you watch a movie or something?"

"Why don't you join us?" Natalie asked. She loved spending time with Carrie. She was witty and had such vitality.

"No offense, but I'd rather stay up here and play with Autumn." Carrie guided Natalie toward the door. "And don't worry about anything. I think I'll spend the night so I can have breakfast with her tomorrow morning."

Before Natalie could say another word, she pushed her out into the hall and closed the door. Wondering what the woman was up to, Natalie descended the stairs, to find Travis standing at the bottom, waiting for her.

His smile sent her pulse racing. "Are you ready for our date?"

She walked right into his outstretched arms. "Another movie?"

He kissed her so passionately her knees gave way, and she would have melted into a puddle at his big, booted feet if not for his strong arms holding her. When he broke the kiss, he turned her toward the family room. "We have a baby-sitter for the evening, there's a movie in the DVD player and the popcorn is ready."

"And you arranged for Carrie to baby-sit." When

he nodded, Natalie asked, "What are we watching tonight?"

"You'll see," he said evasively. Once they were seated on the couch, he put his arm around her shoulders and pulled her to his side. "This is a remake of an older movie, but I think you'll enjoy it."

She smiled when he clicked the remote control and *Father of the Bride* came on the big-screen TV. "I love this movie," she exclaimed. "It's one of the few remakes I enjoy."

Kissing the top of her head, Travis smiled. "I'm glad."

For the next two hours, they laughed as Steve Martin did his best to adjust to being replaced as the number one man in his daughter's life. By the end of the movie, Natalie was sniffling.

"It's so touching how much his wife loved him no matter how ridiculous he acted, and how she helped him move on to the next phase of their lives as parents of a married daughter."

"I'm getting an ulcer just thinking about the day I have to walk Autumn down the aisle and take a back seat to some jerk who won't be nearly good enough for her," Trav said, grimacing.

Natalie smiled. "I'm pretty sure every father goes through that."

Trav rose from the couch to take the disc out of the DVD player. Patting his shirt pocket to make sure the ring was still there, he took a deep breath and turned back to face her. It was time to lay it all on the line.

"I've been thinking I'd like it to be that way when Autumn gets married," he said, walking over to stand in front of Natalie.

She smiled. "The big wedding with all the disasters to deal with?"

He shrugged. "I'm sure that will be part of it. But that's not what I meant." Dropping down on one knee, Trav took her left hand in his as he looked into her wide violet eyes. "What I'm about to say I've never said to any other woman, darlin'." He smiled when her eyes grew round. "I love you, Natalie. You own my heart."

Tears spilled down her smooth cheeks. "I love you, too. So very much."

He reached into his pocket and took out the one-carat diamond ring he'd bought at the Royal Jewelers after leaving the TCC meeting. "Natalie Perez, would you do me the honor of becoming my wife? Will you be there with me when I have to adjust to being the father of the bride, and help me move on to the next phase in our life together?"

Holding up the ring, he felt as if time stood still while he waited for her answer. Her hand was trembling in his, but the smile on her face was the most beautiful sight he'd ever seen.

His chest tightened with more emotion than he'd ever dreamed possible when she nodded and whispered, "Yes. There's nothing I want more in life than to be Mrs. Travis Whelan."

"Nothing?" Without further delay, Trav slid the ring onto her finger, then gazed up at her. "I was thinking we might want a little brother or sister for Autumn in a couple of years."

"I would love to have more children," she said, throwing her arms around his shoulders.

"Darlin', I intend to spend the rest of my days making a good life for you and our kids." He kissed her, making sure she had no doubt that she was his. "And I promise that, as long as I have breath left in my body, no one will hurt you or any of our children ever again."

"I know that," she said, touching his cheek with her soft palm. "That's why I came looking for you when I found myself in trouble. Even though I was too stubborn to admit it, I always knew you were my knight in shining armor."

He chuckled. "More like a cowboy in dusty jeans." Brushing her lips with another kiss, he moved to sit on the couch with her in his arms. "What kind of wedding would you like, darlin'? Something small, or a big one with the whole town of Royal in attendance?"

She gave him a smile that sent his blood pressure skyrocketing. "Whatever you want is fine with me. But would you mind if we wait until next winter?"

"Why wait so long?" he asked, disappointed.

As far as he was concerned, he'd like nothing better

than to get married right away. But with Birkenfeld still on the loose, it was probably better to delay the ceremony until after he was safely behind bars.

"We met in winter, we were reunited in winter and I thought it might be nice to start our lives together in winter," she said, smiling.

He nodded. After everything Natalie had been through, she deserved a fairy tale ending just like the ones in all the old movies she loved so much. And if she wanted a winter wedding, that's exactly what he would give her.

"That will allow plenty of time for you to decide what kind of wedding you want and how big," he said, kissing her again. "But I have to warn you. Married or not, I'm going to spend every day and night from now on showing you just how much I love you."

"Starting when?" she asked, smiling.

"Right now, darlin'," he said, grinning as he stood up with her in his arms.

"I like the way you think," she said, laughing.

And true to his word, Trav carried her upstairs and spent the rest the night showing her just how much he would love her for the rest of their lives.

*   *   *   *   *

Watch for the next installment of the
TEXAS CATTLEMAN'S CLUB:
THE STOLEN BABY
Ry Evans is a consummate bachelor and
the best friend of Travis Whelan.
His job is to watch over Trav's sister
and keep her out of trouble. But just one
incredible kiss is about to land this
cowboy in hot water!

BREATHLESS FOR THE BACHELOR
by Cindy Gerard

Coming to you from Silhouette Desire in
February 2004. For a sneak peek,
just turn the page!

One

"If you call me cute one more time, I swear, I'm going to break every bone in your foot."

Ryan Evans lifted a considering brow and gauged the scowl on Carrie Whelan's face across the booth where they sat in the Royal Diner. She meant business. She wasn't just scowling; she was close to breathing fire as hot as the straight, shining length of silky red hair brushing the small shoulders that were stiffened in a pique of anger.

Carrie was way too much fun to tease. Always had been. And hell, at fourteen, she *had* been cute. At twenty-four, however, it was obvious the idea that he—or any man—would regard her that way, rankled.

Sheer orneriness prompted him to push another hot

button. But safety first. He cleared his throat, pulled himself up straighter and very deliberately drew his long legs back under the faded red plastic booth seat so the simmering Ms. Whelan couldn't stomp the three-inch stiletto heel of her designer boots into his instep.

"That time of the month again is it, sweetie?" he asked with the sage and patronizing compassion of a wise and understanding man.

When she growled, he blinked, all innocence and mystified male guile. "What? What'd I say?"

She tilted her head to the side and studied him as if he were a wad of gum she'd like to scrape off the bottom of her boot. "You know, for a man of such reputed and vast experience with women, you know exactly the wrong things to say to impress a lady."

He couldn't help it. He gave it up and grinned. "Oh, so you're a lady now, are you?"

It wasn't all that long ago that little Carrie Whelan—*cute* little Carrie Whelan, his best friend, Travis Whelan's kid sister—had declared to anyone within earshot that she was gonna be a cowboy and she'd have to be dead before anyone would catch her in anything but denim and her cowboy hat and boots.

Well, he could testify for a fact that she was still alive—very much alive—even though she'd traded denim for silk and her worn Ropers for butter soft Italian ankle boots a few years ago.

And yes. She was definitely alive, Ry thought again before he could curb a quick, appreciative glance at the full healthy breasts pushing against the ivory silk of her blouse.

But he wasn't supposed to notice that. He wasn't supposed to notice anything remotely sexy or female about Carrie.

He tugged his hat brim lower over his brow. The problem was, she was right about one thing. She wasn't cute anymore. She was beautiful...super-model gorgeous, in fact, with those snapping hazel eyes, her tall, willow slim body and a mouth that made a man wonder what it would feel like pressed against his bare skin.

Not him, of course. He didn't think of her that way. At least he tried like hell not to.

Frowning, he schooled his gaze to her face again— to those mossy-green eyes—and forced a mandatory return back to surrogate brother role. "What's got your tail in a twist Carrie-bear?"

The look she threw him could have peeled paint off the bumper of his black 4×4 Ranger. "You're worse than my brother," she sputtered and tipped her coffee—muddy tan and loaded with cream and sugar—to her lips. "Neither one of you takes me seriously."

Ry slumped back in the booth, resisting the urge to own up to exactly how serious he *did* take her. How he'd seriously *like* to take her and how she could seriously mess up his head if he didn't herd his thoughts back in the right direction.

"What'd Trav do now?" he asked instead.

"What does he always do? He treats me like a child."

"He loves you," Ry said softly and watched some of the starch ease out of her stiff spine.

She turned those hazel eyes on him. They made him think of wispy, glittering smoke. Like a night fire, embers banked but smoldering.

"What are we doing here?" she asked abruptly and with such earnest inquiry, he sobered.

"Well, the way I remember it," he said carefully, because he didn't want her getting wise to the fact that at Trav's request, Ry had been sticking pretty close to her for the past week or so, "I called to see how you were doing, you said you'd had a long day, wanted to unwind and asked me to meet you here for a cup of coffee."

She was already shaking her head. "No, I don't mean, what are we doing *here,* at the Royal Diner. I mean, what are *we* doing here—you and me? Look at us. It's Saturday night, for Pete's sake. Why aren't we out on the town with our respective dates, drinking champagne—or in your case, your beer of choice," she added with a smarty-pants smile, "and looking forward to a night of hot, passionate se—"

"Hold it right there." He sat up straight, pushing a hand into the space between them.

When she actually shut up, he wiped that same hand over his jaw then resettled his hat. This was territory he had no intention of invading. "I don't think I want to be discussing my love life with you."

"Not to mention, you don't want to discuss *my* love life."

Yeah, he thought grimly, that too. Keeping a protective eye on her in the wake of the danger that Trav's fiancée, Natalie Perez, still faced was the extent of his involvement with Carrie. He still couldn't believe he'd agreed to play watchdog-slash-bodyguard. Just like he couldn't believe they were having this conversation.

"I didn't hear that," he said firmly. "I didn't hear anything about you even having a love life. Because if I did, I'd have to share the info with your brother and then he'd probably feel obligated to kill the messenger—that would be *me*—before he came looking for you. And Lord have mercy on the man who messed with Travis Whelan's little sister."

She shook her head, pushed out a humorless laugh then stared past him out the grease and smoke-coated window of the diner. "You can breathe easy, big guy. There's not much chance of him killing anyone any time soon. Why? You ask. Because I don't *have* a love life, that's why. And *that's* what's got my *tail in a twist*."

Ryan felt a small bead of sweat form on his forehead, beneath his hatband. This conversation was fast getting out of hand. "I don't think I want to hear about this, either."

Oblivious to the squirming he was doing, she met his eyes with such solemn entreaty that he couldn't look away. "Do you have any idea...do you have even a *remote* idea," she repeated for emphasis, "what it's like being twenty-four years old and still a virgin?"

You are about to enter the exclusive, masculine world of the...

The Stolen Baby

Silhouette Desire's powerful miniseries features six wealthy Texas bachelors—all members of the state's most prestigious club—who must unravel the mystery surrounding one tiny baby...and discover true love in the process!

ENTANGLED WITH A TEXAN by Sara Orwig
(Silhouette Desire #1547, November 2003)

LOCKED UP WITH A LAWMAN by Laura Wright
(Silhouette Desire #1553, December 2003)

REMEMBERING ONE WILD NIGHT by Kathie DeNosky
(Silhouette Desire #1559, January 2004)

BREATHLESS FOR THE BACHELOR by Cindy Gerard
(Silhouette Desire #1564, February 2004)

PRETENDING WITH THE PLAYBOY by Cathleen Galitz
(Silhouette Desire #1569, March 2004)

FIT FOR A SHEIKH by Kristi Gold
(Silhouette Desire #1576, April 2004)

Available at your favorite retail outlet.

presents

DYNASTIES: THE DANFORTHS

**A family of prominence...
tested by scandal, sustained by passion!**

Man Beneath the Uniform
by
MAUREEN CHILD
(Silhouette Desire #1561)

He was her protector. But navy SEAL
Zachary Sheriday wanted to be more
than just a bodyguard to sexy scientist
Kimberly Danforth. Was this one seduction
Zachary was duty-bound to deny...?

*Available February 2004
at your favorite retail outlet.*

Coming February 2004
from
SHERI WHITEFEATHER

Cherokee Stranger
(Silhouette Desire #1563)

James Dalton was the kind of man
a girl couldn't help but want.
The rugged stable manager exuded
sex, secrets…and danger. Local waitress
Emily Chapin had some secrets of her own.
The one thing neither could hide was
their burning need for each other!

***Available at your
favorite retail outlet.***

The Stolen Baby

Silhouette Desire's powerful miniseries
features six wealthy Texas bachelors—
all members of the state's most
prestigious club—who set out to unravel
the mystery surrounding one tiny baby...
and discover true love in the process!

This newest installment continues with

Breathless for the Bachelor
by
CINDY GERARD
(Silhouette Desire #1564)

Meet Ry Evans—consummate bachelor and
best friend of Travis Whelan. His job is to watch
over Trav's sister and keep her out of trouble.
But just one incredible kiss is about to land
this cowboy in hot water!

Available February 2004 at your favorite retail outlet.

COMING NEXT MONTH

#1561 MAN BENEATH THE UNIFORM—Maureen Child
Dynasties: The Danforths
When Navy SEAL Zachary Sheriday was assigned to act as a
bodyguard to feisty Kimberly Danforth, he never considered he'd
be so drawn to his charge. Fiercely independent, and sexy, as well,
Kimberly soon had this buttoned-down military hunk completely
undone. But was this seduction one he was duty-bound to deny…?

#1562 THE MARRIAGE ULTIMATUM—Anne Marie Winston
Kristin Gordon had tried everything possible to get the attention of her
heart's desire: Dr. Derek Mahoney. But Derek's past haunted him, and
made him unwilling to act on the desire he felt for Kristin. Until one
steamy kiss set off a hunger that knew no bounds.

#1563 CHEROKEE STRANGER—Sheri WhiteFeather
He was everything a girl could want. James Dalton, rugged stable
manager, exuded sex…and danger. And for all her sweetness, local
waitress Emily Chapin had secrets of her own. One thing was
perilously clear: their burning need for each other!

#1564 BREATHLESS FOR THE BACHELOR—Cindy Gerard
Texas Cattleman's Club: The Stolen Baby
Sassy Carrie Whelan had always been a little in love with Ry Evans.
But as her big brother's best friend, Ry wasn't having it…until Carrie
decided to pursue another man. Suddenly the self-assured cowboy was
acting like a jealous lover and would do *anything* he could to make
Carrie his.

#1565 THE LONG HOT SUMMER—Rochelle Alers
The Blackstones of Virginia
Dormant desires flared the moment single dad Ryan Blackstone
laid eyes on Kelly Andrews. The sultry beauty was his son's teacher,
and Kelly's gentle manner was winning over both father and son. A
passionate affair with Kelly would be totally inappropriate…and
completely inescapable.

#1566 PLAYING BY THE BABY RULES—Michelle Celmer
Jake Carmichael considered himself a conscientious best friend. So
when Marisa Donato said she wanted a baby without the complications
of marriage, he volunteered to be the father. Their agreement was no
strings attached. But once pent-up passions ignited, those reasonable
rules were quickly thrown out the bedroom window!

SDCNM0104